a

CRADLE AND SPADE.

VOL. I.

CRADLE AND SPADE.

BY

WILLIAM SIME,

AUTHOR OF "KING CAPITAL," "THE RED ROUTE."

VOL. I.

LONDON:

SWAN SONNENSCHEIN, Le BAS & LOWREY,

PATERNOSTER SQUARE.

1886.

Printed by Hazell, Watson, & Viney, Ld., London and Aylesbury.

CONTENTS TO VOL. I.

CRADLE AND SPADE.

CHAPTER I.

CNOC DHU.

Cnoc Dhu, in the spring of 186—, was twenty miles from anywhere. True, it had snowy neighbours, caverned, peaked, blown upon by the blasts of heaven and the sea, like itself; but they were as far away from anywhere as Cnoc Dhu. The hares, the sheep, and red-deer of half-a-dozen mountains round about Cnoc Dhu were nearly the only spectators of the pageantry of spring and the seasons, as it unfolded its wonders among valley and gorge. Nearly, but not quite, for to Elspeth Gun the spring of this year had already revealed itself in a handful of primroses at the side of the burn, which roared down the craggy sides of Cnoc Dhu, past her father's shieling in the hollow of a shelving rock. For a week the burn had not been foaming and tumbling so noisily; the ice had all gone by, and the air was soft and sweet. It was a welcome change to the girl, who wanted to augment her father's larder with some trout, and who, having set lines where the burn joined the Rudder in a valley at the foot of the mountain, had been lucky to the number of half a dozen. But though she felt spring in the air, the girl was not so ungrateful to her mountain as to complain of his winter moods. He had given them violent winds, lightning and thunder and ice, all winter; but that was only Cnoc Dhu's way! Elspeth was used to it, and she was grateful to spring without being ungracious to its predecessor. To see her skip up the sheep-walk which led to the door of the shieling one could see in her lightness of foot, as she ascended,

that she was agreeably conscious of the change. Yes
it was time for the birds to sing again and the lambs
to frisk among the heather; Elspeth felt it in the air,
and she turned on the side of Cnoc Dhu to gaze into
the horizon of peaks beyond the valley of the Rudder,
and it was a pity there was nothing better to see her
than a hawk who was wheeling towards an invisible
victim among the moors. Elspeth Gun bore the
mark in her face of being twenty miles from anywhere. She had a gentle mournfulness of expression
in her eyes of still grey which had come to her face
from no inward sorrow, only from the communion
with high craigs and birds of the moor and un-
visited waters. But she carried herself in a stalwart
style, and there was something of the wild-deer in
her manner as she threw back from her brow the
luxuriance of her harvest-coloured hair to scan the
invisible things of the distance. She saw spring
everywhere, and turning, hastened towards the
shieling, light of heart and with a song on her lips.

It was the work of a few minutes for her to clean
her trout and give them over to her mother for the
shepherd's meal when he descended Cnoc Dhu in the
evening. They were the first of the early year, and
she was pleased to think of her father's pleasure as
she hastened again to the burn with a basin. Her
errand this time was only to gather a dish of sand,
and she found the sand in a ridge where the over-
flowing stream had left it. To-morrow was to be a
great day in the shieling. All the woodwork was
to be polished until it shone. Rafters were to be
rubbed until the smoke had vanished. Everything
which could take on the hue of cleanliness would
be required to do so; hence Elspeth's sand. When
Oliver Gun, the shepherd, followed by a couple of
collies, and carrying a staff, came into the shieling,
he learned that a dish of trout awaited him, and it
was with more than usual complaisance that he unwound a plaid from his shoulders, took off his coat,
and, gathering a handful of Elspeth's sand, began to

make himself fit company for his evening at home. Sand is a rough sort of soap at any time, but Oliver seemed to find his handful rougher than usual.

"Lassie," he said, looking into the basin where he had been chafing one hand against another, "where got ye this? It's liker shingle than sand. You must have dipped your dish to the bottom of the burn for it."

"There's nothing the matter with it, father," said Elspeth, taking up a handful to show how freely she could use it; "it's rather finer sand than I'm used to take into the house. It's the sand that the burn has washed up of its own accord. It has to polish all our rafters."

The shepherd said no more; he only abandoned Elspeth's soap, and going outside he thrust his massive head and straw-coloured beard beneath a spout in the rock, whence a stream of water descended into a pool at the side of the burn. He was gasping freely and holding out his hand for a towel, which his wife was offering him, when Elspeth came to the shieling door, and peered into the hollow of her right palm.

"Father, no wonder you cried out," said the girl, stirring some object with her forefinger. "Look what's in the sand. It's full of it."

The shepherd having dried his ample face, looked into Elspeth's palm. Mrs. Gun, equally interested in the discovery, peered over her husband's elbow, and lent him her ring-finger, as he grasped it, without a word, to compare the gold hoop with the shining particles which his daughter held out.

"Na, na," said Mrs. Gun, "it's no the same thing;" her husband triumphantly but silently keeping the raw and manufactured metal in proximity.

"Christina Gun," said the shepherd, at length, "it *is* the same thing. It's red gold, and there's enough of it in Elspeth's palm to marry her with. There is that."

"There's plenty more in the basin, then," said

Elspeth. "Take your noses out of my hand, collie dogs, it's nothing for you. Yes, father, the basin's full of it."

"It's just trash," said Mrs. Gun, putting her trout on the fire, and turning her back upon the follies of father and daughter, the former having lifted the basin to the door with the caution he might have used to a young lamb.

"What do ye think, lassie?" asked the shepherd, a little shaken in his opinion by his wife's contemptuous scepticism.

"I couldn't say, father; maybe ay and maybe no; for I have no knowledge of gold."

"Fling it out o' your hands, Oliver Gun, gold or no gold, what have we to do with it? It's the root of all evil, if it is gold," cried Mrs. Gun, setting her table with her dish of trout and pouring out her husband's tea. "What would you say, Elspeth?"

"I should say, no, don't fling it out. It's a gift to us from the 'good people,' and if we give the fairies offence for not taking what they bring us, their next gift mayn't be so nice a one. Many's the thing what is made of gold, mother, besides a marriage ring. Did ye never look into the jeweller's window in the High Street of Ruddersdale? Well, and didn't ye see 'drops' for the ears, chains for the wrist, and pins for the throat? Mother, ye have no eyes when ye go to Ruddersdale. Many's the time in my dreams that window has appeared to me and I was putting out my hand to choose, would it be this one or would it be that one I would take to wear in my ears or on my breast——"

"Elspeth, you are forgetting yourself. Go out round about to the stack, and bring half a dozen peats for the fire. Oliver, sit down to your supper; they're fine tasty trout. The lassie's demented."

"Ay; but it's a little lonesome for a fine lass like Elspeth never to be off Cnoc Dhu, Christina Gun; never to be seeing nothing but an empty valley and hearing the plovers. It's no good for her, and next time I go into Ruddersdale Elspeth comes with me, to get a look in at her jeweller's window, and to buy a blue ribbon for her hair."

"Oh, fill her head with notions, Oliver Gun. Put brooches and earrings and men into her head, and——"

Elspeth entered with an armful of peats and deposited them at the side of the fire. Then she took up the saucer, into which Oliver had poured the shining particles."

"Lassie," said the shepherd, "I'm going to Ruddersdale to-morrow. D'ye think ye could win that far on your feet? We would start early in the morning—before daybreak—and we would stay all night at Nancy Harper's, and come away before daybreak the day after."

"Is it the gold, Oliver?" asked Mrs. Gun, anxiously.

"No; it's the sheep; but there's no harm in taking the parcel with us."

"Elspeth Gun, you're a well-off girl," said the mother; "it's not many lassies in the town what has fathers that spoil them, I can tell ye."

"Well, father, I'll go," said the girl, hastening to open a box in her little room at the back of the shieling, and to sew gum-flowers upon a hat. "I'll go and see what it is the fairies have sent us."

Long before the clouds had risen from the mountains, father and daughter were on their way to Ruddersdale next morning. Oliver was so used to the face of Cnoc Dhu that he could have climbed to its summit blindfold, and Elspeth knew every twist and turn of the valley of the Rudder for six miles from her father's door. They neither stumbled nor spoke until daylight appeared, and by that time they were on the edge of the "strath," or valley of the stream, at the first bridge and road which crossed it. They halted there and breakfasted on bannocks and cheese, the valley lightening around them with lambent flames of red and gold, which gave to the gurgling Rudder an aspect of molten fire.

"It's like to be stormy after a time," said Elspeth, who knew the signs of the heavens, "but it's a noble river it makes of the Rudder. You would think it was all gold this morning." The shepherd felt in his waistcoat pocket, took out a snuff-box, saw that the particles were safe, and said, "I hope Mr. Leslie won't laugh at us, Elspeth. If it's only the dust of brass, as your mother says, and not gold at all, we'll have had a long walk for little. But I have my own notions as well as your mother. I rather suppose that brass isn't found that way. Your mother's a wee thing opinionative. Let's be off again." And, single file, they set off again, walking mile after mile without any diversion more exciting than the rush of Oliver's collie at a cock-grouse, or a momentary stop to look at a kestrel wheeling from the crags of the river, or a pause of the shepherd to criticise the flocks. It was well on in the forenoon when they got within breathing of the sea. Elspeth adjusted her petticoats and arranged her hat, and said, " Father, now put on your bonnet right, we'll be meeting some o' the town's folks. Oh, I see the ocean; I haven't looked on the face of it since I was last on the top of Cnoc Dhu! Oh, father, the ships and the white sails—and the waves breaking on the beach!"

Ruddersdale did not, perhaps, contain more than 1,500 people, yet it presented to the shore a handsome open square of houses. Neither Elspeth nor her mother had ever seen a larger township. Oliver at times had followed his flocks to various country towns beyond the mountains, and naturally knew life; yet he spoke below his breath as his daughter and he came into the square, telling her to wait outside Mr. Leslie's bank while he asked the banker's opinion about the contents of the snuff-box. It was no small trial for the shepherd to push aside the lofty folding doors of the bank, and to find himself fronted by half a dozen young gentlemen of the town, who gazed at him peremptorily, and with the air of being absolute owners of the strong box. Certainly, it was rather an impertinence, for a shepherd, with a staff and a collie who declined to be left outside, to ask for Mr. Leslie, even though he put his request with a humble voice and demeanour. For Mr. Leslie, seated in his own room behind the clerks, was unapproachable except to some of the larger graziers of the shore and the sheep-farmers who rode in to superintend shipments at the pier.

"I cannot tell you what it is, but I must see himself," Oliver remarked, half a dozen times in reply to a question which was six times asked. Whereupon the young gentlemen turned to their ledgers, and he was left standing until the inner door opened, and a man, with an exceedingly red face and a pair of bloodshot eyes, looked out. Few shepherds came to the bank. Mr. Leslie was struck with the aspect of the man who waited to see him.

"What does he want?" he called out. "Come round here, man. Well, come in then to my room. What the deuce are you doing? I don't want the door shut."

Mr. Leslie was a man on a colossal scale of stoutness; he was booted and spurred, and ready to take a journey, as Oliver noticed; but he shut the door.

"Now be quick about it, shepherd, whatever it is you have to tell. Mail coach leaves this way in a short time, and I'm due on the top."

Oliver took out his snuff-box.

"Never mind the mull, I don't snuff. There's three minutes at your disposal to tell me what you are here for."

"Mr. Leslie," said the shepherd, pouring the yellow particles upon the mahogany edge of a table, "what's that?"

The banker swept the dust into the palm of his hand, weighed it, smelt it, put it on a pair of minute scales on his mantel-piece.

"About fifteen shillings' worth of gold-dust," he said, "you might have handed that over to one of my clerks. I suppose you've had it from some returned digger—an old Ballarat man for example."

"No, sir, that gold was picked off the side of Cnoc Dhu."

"Impossible! There's no gold on Cnoc Dhu. I tell ye, ye got that dust from an old Ballarat man. Let me know a little more about gold than you. And you might as well expect to get peaches on a cabbage-stack as gold out of a peat bog. You're a simple fellow, man. That's gold from Ballarat, and if ye want fifteen shillings for it, ye can get it."

"Mr. Leslie," said the shepherd, "I'm not so very much needing your fifteen shillings; but I never tell a lie except when I can't help it, and then it's necessary; and as sure as God made me that gold was found in the valley of the Rudder, among the sand, and if there's fifteen shillings' worth there's more where it came from."

The huge banker said nothing, but carried the scales to the window and peered closely at the contents.

"Gold at Cnoc Dhu," he murmured, "gold at Cnoc Dhu. Never heard of the ghost of a legend of such a thing. But I've noticed veins of quartz and quantities of granite over there, any time these twenty years. It may be. Look here, my man. Here's a gold sovereign for your nieveful of dust. You can keep a secret, I suppose. Now, if there's gold at Cnoc Dhu, that's a secret of some little importance, and it was very right and proper of you to come to me, the factor of that hill-range, first and foremost. You might have gone to a fool of a watchmaker who would have dropped half the dust on the floor and given you back the other half with an offer of ninepence. Ye hear me, it's a secret, and ye are to keep it, and one of these fine afternoons you will meet me at the wooden bridge and show me where this stuff was picked up. Ye did quite right to ask to see me. What infernal scraping at the door is that? Oh, that is your dog, is it? Now, shepherd, not a word, not a single word to a human being in Ruddersdale. Back you go to your mountain and your sheep, and meet me at the bridge on the fourth afternoon from this, at half-past three o'clock."

Oliver went out into the square and said nothing to his daughter as they walked from the square into the little street of thatched houses, where Nancy Harper's sign was. He said nothing as Nancy, with a black cap on her head, welcomed them within her kitchen bar. But in the evening, when Elspeth and he walked down the stout, stone pier, and stood within the lee of its outer wall, he took out his red handkerchief and furtively showed her a sovereign, shining like a sunset.

CHAPTER II.

PARLIAMENT HOUSE.

JOSEPH NIXON, in the spring of the same year, stood
one afternoon, with a gigantic advocate's wig in his
right hand, at the foot of a statue in the Parliament
House of Edinburgh. The great hall of justice was
full of suitors, and from the several doorways leading
to the outer and inner courts, men with keen, sallow
faces were bending a listening ear to other men with
faces of a similar caste and hue, who coached them
as they sauntered. Nobody coached Joseph, and an
incident had only then occurred which made it pro-
bable that it would be some considerable time before
he was approached in that confidential manner by a
small man, with a handful of blue paper tied with a

ribbon. Joseph had been entrusted with the conduct
of a case in the Outer House, and he had been
expected to make a speech of some length, under
the sarcastic nose of a wizened gentleman in a
wig. He had been expected to address the wizened
gentleman as " M'Lud," whereas, when he stood up
he said " M' Lor-r-rd," in a broad, plain accent.
He could not for the life of him achieve the mincing
language of the law, and " M'Lud's " surprise was so
pronounced at the unwonted sound that he took the
opportunity of interrupting Joseph, and of saying,
" Mr. Nixon, you are a master of R's, are you
not? Very good. Proceed." The laughter among
the lawyers so discomfited the advocate that he had
to begin again at " M' Lor-r-rd," which the judge,
interpreting as the attempt of a young pleader to
establish a manner of his own, snubbed a second
time by the question, " Mr. Nixon, have you looked
at your brief before you came into this court? I
can tell you I have something else to do than listen

to the raw, unprepared utterances——" "M' Lor-r-rd,"
interrupted Nixon, in an agony, for the Writer to the
Signet who had retained him was frowning at the
foot of the witness-box, and the opposition advocate
was standing, in the attitude of a teapot, with
triumph on every lineament. The consequence was
that Joseph Nixon, surprised out of all knowledge
of his brief, contributed nothing to its elucidation
but "eh—ah—ah—eh"; and the judge, who was
exceedingly hungry, gathered up his robes and left
him stammering. For three long years had Nixon
wandered up and down the great hall waiting for
his opportunity. It had come at last, and that was
the ignominious result. He had been "left speaking"
with a vengeance. Yet it was with no feeling of
having been humbled that he stood at the foot of
the statue, holding his wig by the strings as if it
were a sling. He felt that he had not got fair
play, and though his kind of snubbing had been
experienced, one way and another, by most of the

occupants of the hall, from the mouth of the same judge, it was none the less bitter to him.

"Nixon, how d'ye like it?" asked a jeering voice from the other side of the statue. "We've all had to go through it, my boy. He's the prince of curmudgeons."

"He's a brute-beast," said Nixon. "I'll never put a wig on again. I deliberately take the infamous top-piece off in the face of this august assembly of sharks, and I don't know what hinders me from kicking it from end to end of the place. Faugh! the miserable emblem of justice, manufactured from——"

"I say, Nixon, old fellow, why are you unrobing in that premature and savage manner?" asked another brother of the wig and gown, who had laughed consumedly in the Outer House when he saw the judge retire like an old lady in a dudgeon.

"I tell you, I'm not going to stand it," repeated Nixon, whose ruffled hair and expression of incon-

tinent protest seemed · to grow upon the strollers of
the law, who passed and repassed, for there was a
prevailing tendency to look at him and to laugh.
He was standing with his gown unbuttoned when
a young advocate, with keen black eyes, and a chin
with an appearance of suppressed ebony about it,
came rapidly towards him. He had just come out
of the Inner House, where he had been junior in an
important case to the Solicitor-General. The flush
of success was on his cheek as he thrust his hand
into Nixon's arm and exclaimed,—

"Joe, for Heaven's sake, don't look so simply and
naturally indignant. The faculty can't afford to have
its youngest member wear an expression so com-
pletely in unison with the emotions of his bosom.
My dear fellow, screw up the muscles of your face
and get out an expression of calm indifference. I've
heard about your little—eh?—collapse. Never mind.
Better luck next time. He's the prince of curmudgeons."

"Oh, is he? I suppose that phrase is meant to stick—has been dropped by the epigrammatic Bob, and——. No, I shan't put the wig on, Usher. I take it off and abandon it for ever. Unhand me, you sinner; I get out of my gown also, and now I am a free man, Heaven be thanked."

" Better to have pled and failed than never to have pled at all," said the successful Usher, looking at his liberated friend, who stood six feet, the most unlawyer-like of men, abler to split rails it appeared, from the mass of his right arm, than to chop logic, a very Hercules of muscular force, with a face of child-like openness and unreserve. At that moment the great friend of Usher sauntered by; then he turned and looked at Nixon, standing, gown and wig over his left arm. He had a telegram in his hand, which he opened as he approached.

"Nixon, my man, you should try this," he said; "you'll be in a more lucrative field than the Inner House affords. Discovery of gold among the mountains of Cnoc Dhu, away at the Marnock Firth. Some samples already taken. No doubt about it. I always thought there was gold to be got in Scotland—look at King Jamie's bonnet-pieces—if they could only hit it. An infant like that," pursued the Solicitor-General, walking away with his hand on Usher's arm, "has no right to belong to the profession. It was a real kindness to him to suppress him at his first brief."

Nixon went home to his rooms, and, having dined, he made a sort of inventory of all he possessed. Having done so, he looked out a bunch of bills and tried to see his way through them. To meet them and be an undebted man he found that he would have to part with nearly everything he had collected during his years of preparation for the Scotch bar. His resources were at an end. His career, which promised to start that day, was ended too.

" My canoe. Yes, my canoe will meet that," he said, laying a light boat on his dining-room table, and fixing a boot-maker's account to it. "My rifle; yes, I think it is good for all I owe here," he said, bringing the nipple down upon his tailor's bill. "My rod, my trusty wand, which has shaken in the wind of so many streams, how can I part with it, even to meet the pressing claims of my tobacconist? And my trusty pocket-book, filled with lures, in which the abandoned odour of a bank-note has never been known, how can I hand you over to a grocer? Stripped, stripped naked, as when I first came into the world without gown, without wig, without brief, I, Joseph Nixon, must start out in search of bread. Well, haven't I got a biceps?"

"I say, Nixon, what have you tumbled your rooms about for?" asked Usher's voice at his dining-room door; "and who are you apostrophizing? Are you rehearsing your 'M'Luds' for the next occasion?"

Usher pushed his way past the projecting canoe and the intrusive fishing-rod, tumbled over the rifle, and stood with his hands on the shoulders of his friend.

"No," said Nixon, "you'll never see me in that old Parliament House again. It is farewell law and all the curmudgeons. By the way, Usher, you see this stand of golf-clubs; d'ye know anybody who'd be likely to offer a respectable sum for them?" And Nixon pinned a bookseller's account to a golf-ball.

"Joe, what's all this? You are the veriest old entomologist gone cracked. You ticket your valuables with an account, one after another. I don't understand it."

"It's this, Usher, that I am obliged to fall back upon my biceps. I'm not wanted at the Parliament House. Perhaps I can help to lay a railway. Anyhow, I needn't subject myself to a repetition of the insult of to-day, or wait for another three years on the off-chance of being allowed to subject myself to it. I am done with it."

Usher drew himself back to the fireplace and looked narrowly at his friend, who distributed all his bills in silence.

"Yes, I think I shall have enough to cover everything before I shake the dust off my feet and go out to measure my biceps against mother earth."

"Are you going to be a gravedigger, Joe?"

"Take your fun out of it, Usher. Laugh away, lad. You laugh best because you laugh last."

"And—and——" said Usher, looking intently into his companion's face, "what account of it will you give to the sheriff's ward? I suppose you haven't altered anyway in your feeling about her?"

"Usher, you ought to know me better than to suppose that my alteration of fortune means any change of feeling. No, my old confederate, I am as much a slave to her every look and nod as I have been these three years."

"And yet you take off your gown and your wig and toss away all your professional prospects at the first fit of indigestion which meets you on the Bench. You lay down your hopes of honourable success, and —Nixon, you're an infant."

"Well, be it so ; but it has been growing on me that my place is not at the bar, that I will get grey there, and yet have achieved nothing. Besides, you see these bills—they must be met. My supplies are permanently stopped in as mysterious a style as ever they originated. It is a *pis-aller*."

Usher looked at his friend complaisantly. He did not seem to regret his mishap of the day. He appeared rather to enjoy his embarrassment. In relation to the girl he alluded to as the sheriff's ward, he showed no feeling but that of curiosity. Nixon, however, did not read his manner in that light. Rather he thought, Usher had hardened into a cynical questioner, and, that his surface manner had nothing to do with his inward feeling.

"You don't know, I suppose, that the sheriff was sitting in the Outer House to-day, when you—eh ? "

"I am more than sorry to hear it. I had hoped to give him my own version of the breakdown, and my own explanation."

"They tell me he looked devilish cut up. Not that he was ever much of a pleader himself. But, Nixon, you know he had set his heart upon a man for that ward of his who could plead her mysterious cause through all the courts of the empire if it were necessary. Now he knows you can't do it. My boy, I am sorry I can't administer the comfort to you which you, perhaps, deserve. It's a crisis for you. Everything seems down on you. The very stars are fighting in their courses against you."

"That'll do, Usher, thanks. I can bear my own misfortunes without either your sympathy or your rhetoric. But I *am* sorry the sheriff happened to hear and see what a miserable breakdown it was. I shall call on him."

"And on her?"

"Naturally, I shall see her, when I go to Corstorphine. Usher, you have stood my friend once and again. Give me your hand that you will stand my friend in my absence, that when I am out of it and fighting elsewhere, you will, as far as you can, help me against rivals with her."

Usher smiled. He did not choose to hold a brief for the friend he knew best in the world, when it meant making speeches in his praise to the most popular girl known to the inhabitants of the Courts.

"I suppose, Nixon, there is no doubt you are the prime favourite with her; that, in fact, you consider yourself engaged to her, and all that sort of thing."

"Yes, and all that sort of thing," said Nixon, bitterly.

"Well, you certainly are 'down on your luck,' as the saying of the vulgar is; for if her marriage depends upon the old sheriff, you believe me, his face to-day indicated anything but consent."

"She won't ask him. She oughtn't to ask on such a subject—a thing that may affect her whole life."

"Undoubtedly it will; and, Nixon, how much did you say you would sell your golf-sticks for? I don't mind offering five guineas for the set. It isn't much, but, poor Joe, if you are going out of it, I shall like to have a swing at Musselburgh with your clique; and five guineas is all I can afford."

"Have them as a gift," said Nixon; "I'll make my landlady send them round to-night. Hang it, there are plenty of things here to pay out all the creditors. The canoe, I daresay, I will get £20 from Tom Mackenzie for, though it has been in every western inlet and up every eastern river in old Scotland."

"Poor Joe!" said Usher, looking with something like a glance of affection at him, "you are a stormy petrel, at home on the ocean, in your element rushing over a Scotch rapid, happy when you are puffing at a tough mountain precipice. I don't know what to suggest to you. In love with the sheriff's ward—ward presumably in love with you—sheriff not so sure about it as he ought to be—your funds run out—snubbed in the Outer House—another fellow got the brief. Toss wig in the air—future as blank as John Locke's sheet of paper. I cannot advise, my dear friend. There are no precedents to apply to your case."

"I will go up to the Corstorphine Hill and see my true love," said the disrobed giant.

"Well, if you are consoled in that quarter, you are independent of every other consolation," said Usher.

And so Nixon went out to Corstorphine Hill next day, on the seaward side of which Sheriff Durie's house, approached by an avenue, and surrounded by a rookery, looked towards the distant Firth. He felt unaccountably like a tramp as he passed up the avenue, or a burglar who had designs upon the silver. For the resolution to lay aside his gown and wig, and to front the remainder of his life with his right arm as his chief weapon, had opened new vistas for

him. What to do with that right arm of his? No
doubt it was the brawniest and strongest, and contained a great quantity of latent force; and if going
about with it, to knock down Writers to the Signet,
could have solved the problem of his fortunes, then
there would have been no difficulty. But that was
a closed career; so was prize-fighting, or any of the
elementary professions dependent upon primitive
force of muscle. It is to be feared that, as the
sheriff's man showed him into the drawing-room, he
did not look so reputable as he had hitherto done
when he visited Durie Den. He was mighty anxious
to know about the sheriff, whether he was at home,
whether he would be likely to be back soon, and
whether Miss Durie had accompanied him round
Corstorphine on horseback? And being told that
the sheriff was riding alone, he almost gasped with
satisfaction.

CHAPTER III.

THE SHERIFF'S WARD.

MISS DURIE came in presently, and shook hands
with him. The sheriff's ward seemed not less anxious
to see Nixon without the intervention of the sheriff
than he was himself. She was a slight, rather fragile-
looking creature, with the deceptive air of a physical
weakness which she did not feel, and had never felt.
Not that she affected the air of languor or fatigue
due to physical depression; rather her air was of
one who, being fragile, overcame it by force of will.
She was a noticeable girl, for the poise of her head
and the columnar neck which carried it. Her hair
was worn, as a boy's might be, in brief ripples of
the glossiest black; her face had an expression of

mischievous openness, the eyes containing, in their pronounced darkness, the possibilities of strong alternations of love and hate. There was nothing to remark about her nose beyond the fact of its being " tip-tilted "; and her mouth was rather wider than perfect mouths ought to be, but it was mobile, and capable of expressing, with great rapidity, the thoughts and feelings which agitated her.

"Mina," said Nixon, finding a gentler use for the right arm than that of felling Writers to the Signet, and advancing with her towards the window, "it will have to be postponed. We cannot marry yet awhile. I have no prospect in the Parliament House; the judge has extinguished me. I can never hope to recover myself."

Mina had heard the story of Joseph's discomfiture, and had shed more tears than she would ever be likely to confess to as the sheriff went over the scene. He had made it very ludicrous as he told of the contemptuous judge and the indignant solicitor, and

Nixon standing with his jaws unable to articulate a word, and the bystanders laughing. But he had been very earnest a little later on, pointing out to his ward that such a man as Joseph, though he had certain attractions about him, being a fine oarsman, an accomplished shot, a climber, a boxer and what not, was devoid of the stuff which he desired to see a lover of hers to possess. Mina knew that the sheriff was thinking of Usher, who had ridden out a good deal to Durie Den with Nixon, and who, quite without Nixon's knowing it, had made a great deal of love to her. For Usher was the sheriff's ideal of a young man destined to succeed at the bar, and, as he was always telling her, "Mina, you will greatly want an advocate."

"Joe, dear, I have heard it all from poor papa; he was much cut up about it. He heard you, you know."

"I wish he had. The trouble of it is, I hadn't a word to say for myself. I couldn't open my mouth.

I was so caught at the throat by the sight of that old judge, sardonically drawing his nostrils together, or preparing to rise and retire on the first provocation, that I had the sensation of choking. He might have helped a fellow through with his first brief. But it's all over now, dear; no more briefs for me. My reputation is gone at all the shops. Not a Writer to the Signet would entrust me even with a notice of motion at a couple of guineas down."

Mina liberated herself from Nixon's arm, and inclined her ear towards the lodge at the end of the avenue. The sheriff was returning. There he was, shaking his whip at his ward. He did not see Nixon. He would be with them in a few minutes.

"But Joe, dear," said the girl, "is that failure such a serious thing for you? Don't you know all the saws about trying, till, like Bruce's spider, you put yourself into your native spot?"

"And so I would try again, and again, and again,

and again, if I didn't feel that, somehow, I am on a wrong tack at the bar. I shall never bring in my little boat there. The sheriff!"

It was the sheriff, and he did not look particularly cordial, as Nixon approached him with an extended arm. He looked anxiously towards his ward, and from her to the lover, whom he was obliged to tolerate, because Mina liked him.

"I congratulate you, I'm sure, Nixon," he said, "on your first brief. Highly satisfactory—very. I suppose the Writers to the Signet are mobbing you, and burying you under deeds."

"You are a little severe, sheriff," said Nixon, who, being emancipated from law, felt the glory of his independence, and was not inclined to be chaffed. Then a silence fell upon the room, Mina stooping to turn over a footstool, the sheriff pulling his beard, Nixon feeling that he was one too many.

The silence, after a little, became so painful to the girl that she rose and quietly closed the door behind her, leaving the men alone. Sheriff Durie was a small, neat man, with a silky beard and two penetrating eyes. As he passed his hands through the hair of his chin, he looked shrewdly at Nixon, and waited for a remark. None came, however, so he opened the conversation himself.

"Nixon," he said, "I'm sorry for your little misfortune. It will take you some time to repair it, and you are poor. Do you still propose to hold Mina to her word?"

"If the girl loves me as I love her, she will not want compulsion. She will wait for me."

"She will wait. Ah, you young fellows! You talk of marrying the girl out of my house as if there were nothing in it but a question of personal convenience to yourself. Don't you know that I have made her my daughter; that I have watched over her these sixteen years with an affection which has gone on growing, and that I grudge her—ay, every look of her—to anybody else?"

Nixon knew the fatherly esteem in which the sheriff held the girl, but there was something in the tone of his complaint which seemed to suggest that he grudged her to another, because the paternal esteem had passed into a different order of feeling. He might have been a rival, so fiery was his protest; and looking at him, Nixon for the first time saw that if he chose to be a rival he would not be contemptible on the score of looks.

The sheriff read what was passing in the young man's mind, and with a softer intonation than he had used, he went on,—

"She is the only daughter, Nixon, which Heaven has been good enough to send me, and she has done so much to make life tolerable for me, that I feel myself bound to guard her with the utmost jealousy. I must, indeed, before I allow her to pass from the protection of my roof, be assured that she is not going to share hardship and penury. You understand me, therefore, when I put to you the plain question, Do you still propose to keep her to her word ? "

"I should like to keep her to nothing that would lessen her happiness, sheriff."

" That's well said, Nixon, and I'm inclined to think that you feel as you speak. Now, Mina is a girl who has not been sent into the world to rough it. She will at all times require at least such surroundings—poor though they are—as I have given her here."

Nixon looked hopelessly out upon the lawn at the blackbirds carrying bits of hay for their nests among the hollies, and wondered when he would be able to offer her "such surroundings."

" Besides," pursued the sheriff, " before Mina marries, I should like to find out what her name is. Durie will do in the meantime. It is the name I have been pleased she should take, in lieu, perhaps, of a better. Of course, Mina has told you her story. You know how she came to be ward of mine ; how, during one of my sittings in the North, she was rescued among the cruel Northern breakers, and how, being brought ashore, I took charge of her and all her worldly possessions, as they survived, and were handed over to me. These consisted of three fragments of a deed, amounting to a sum total of one sentence, out of which the most skilful heads of the law in this metropolis have been unable to make a possibility of meaning. By long study, however, by judicious conjecture, by questioning of the people who brought me Mina sixteen years ago, I have constructed a theory. Wait a minute; I will fetch you these fragments of a deed, and you can look at them for yourself. Here they are, three sibyl-leaves, and nobody to interpret them. Why they should be torn ribbons of parchment like that, I am at a loss to know. Obviously, as even you, a single-brief man, may see, the ribbons belong to an entire deed. If that deed were discovered, I make no doubt that Mina Durie would turn out to be a woman of

fortune, daughter to somebody of very great consequence in some part of the world, but what part
even I cannot tell. I was inclined, at one time, to
attribute her to this nation, and again to that, and
a third time to a third; I have had skilled ethno-
logists of the Royal Society here, who, without Mina
knowing it, have studied every feature of her face,
every conformation of her head, and who have given
it up in despair. To-day I am no nearer the goal
than I was sixteen years ago. Perhaps I am not
so anxious as I once was to solve the mystery, for I
dread, as you know, another claimant. If, however,
Mina is to be married, I shall care for her destined
husband interesting himself in her origin. Indeed,
I will go further, and say to you, Nixon, that I shall
expect any young man who seriously asks her hand
to devote some years of his life to looking for the
remainder of this deed. Go out into the world,
Nixon, solve that problem, and you shall be the most
welcome guest which Durie Den ever entertained,

when you come back successful. There will then be no need to regret the collapse of the first brief."

Nixon leant over to the sheriff and took the three strips of the deed. There was nothing characteristic about the stuff the writing appeared upon; there was no clue to anything in the few English words which seemed to be devising property to somebody. The advocate handed them back with a gesture of despair.

"I, too," he said, "have a problem to solve. As yet I don't know how I came here. The mystery of my own origin first drew me to Mina, and it was comparing notes about the strangeness of the circumstance which made us feel that, in some other sphere, we must have been destined for each other."

"Mr. Nixon, that's the sort of rubbish which we may expect to hear in a romance. Man to man, however, it is little use indulging in allusions to the spheres. Marriages are made on earth and not in heaven, and judging from the average matrimonial felicities it would be a poor compliment to any heavenly committee to suppose that it occupied itself with pairing off men and women in these regions. Besides, my dear sir," said the sheriff, in a brusque, irritated tone, " there was, I believe, some investigation on the part of Joseph Nixon into Joseph Nixon's origin, which, if I am not mistaken, ended in a— ahem—something about a bar-sinister."

Nixon rose in anger, and a warm crimson overspread his face.

"I was advised to drop inquiring," he said. "Nor did it signify much to anybody who Joseph Nixon was, or where he came from, or whether he ever had any parents."

The sheriff was sorry he had wounded the young man.

"Nixon," he said, "I believe Mina has a little partiality for you. Now the best thing you can do to heighten that partiality into love is to devote yourself to her service. What better pursuit can a young fellow, with your legal training and your fighting muscles, have than to win your sweetheart after the high-hearted old fashion of better days than ours? Tell me, are you willing to go through fire and water for her? Then take a strip of that deed and search for the remainder. You have the wide world to find it in, no doubt; but what is that to a man of your years? And chance may help you in your quest, for chance is kind to the venturesome, and tosses them advantages when they are least expecting them. Go, man, and tell me who my ward is."

At that moment Mina entered the room again. She had thrust a little bouquet of primroses into her breast; and the sheriff, looking at her affectionately, said, "You are just in time, Mina. Nixon was rising to go. You won't be likely to see him for—well, I wouldn't like to put a date upon it, Nixon, for it is a longish job. Good-bye, Nixon, go with a stout heart and a steadfast purpose, and the first news of success you have, write me. My address will be Durie Den, always Durie Den."

Joseph rose, feeling that he was being turned out of the house summarily.

Mina looked unhappily at him, and her eyes glistened.

" You go—where ? "

" Ah, it's a secret, Mina, between Joseph and myself. You must make no inquiries. All you have got to do is to shake hands, and say, ' Luck be with you, Joseph,' as indeed I wish him a most fortunate discovery."

" But——" said Joseph, looking at Mina, as if a great gulf had yawned between them.

She glanced from the sheriff's face to the advocate's with a mute look of inquiry. There was no explanation.

The sheriff had touched the right chord in her lover. He had given him a mission, and, as it were, put him upon his honour to satisfactorily accomplish it.

"I will come to the gate with you, Nixon. There isn't much daylight remaining to take you back to Edinburgh, but you will have the stars above your head—excellent, encouraging company to those who understand their celestial winking."

"Good-bye, dear," said Mina, leaning her head for one brief instant on her lover's breast, while the sheriff, going downstairs, called back,—

"I will go with you as far as the gate, Nixon."

"You will be true to me," whispered the advocate, looking down into the sorrowful eyes.

"Yes, dear," replied the girl, releasing him to join the shouting sheriff.

CHAPTER IV.

THE sheriff was brave and cheerful till he got to his lodge gate with Joseph Nixon. He shouted down the road to him:

"Remember, Nixon, with that strip of a deed of conveyance you may do anything. Anything," he added, making a speaking-trumpet of his fist, and raising his voice till it echoed over the hill-side, while Joseph, hearing him as if he were in a dream, neither turned nor responded.

When the sheriff got back, however, to his own door, he had a little sinking at the heart. He did not feel sure that Mina would consider his summary disposal of her lover as so admirable a thing. Indeed, he began to have a foretaste of compromise on the subject, even before he joined the girl in the dining-room. He already saw the impecunious bar-failure restored to favour: for he felt that if Mina were to hold out, he must give in; there was just the chance that the young fellow would himself keep out of sight until time, with its healing influence, put him out of mind. At dinner Mina was not visibly affected. Had the sheriff been more keen-sighted he would, no doubt, have noticed a little ring of darkness under her eyes, which might have indicated a little crying and a little drying. He was in no mood, however, to detect or observe what was not thrust upon his notice, so he contented himself with talking lightly of everything which seemed most remote, by association or suggestion from Joseph Nixon. Warmed by his wine, and replenished by his good three courses, he ventured by-and-by to say:

"Mina, I think of going up to my county this

year. You must come with me. The change will
do you good. There's no particular reason, on the
score of work, why I should go. That sheriff-
substitute is a terrible fellow for judgments. He
never leaves me an opportunity to justify my existence by recalling a single interlocutor. I did it once
to keep my hand in, and the Lords affirmed his
judgment and overruled mine. A burnt child, Mina,
dreads the fire. All the same, I should like to
shoulder a fishing-rod in the field of my jurisdiction;
it would put some colour in your cheeks. Besides,
you are growing curious to see that bit of coast
where they brought you ashore. You and I shall
go and look at it, and see if we can bring ourselves
any nearer the mystery. Who knows, Mina, that the
secret may not be hidden within some of those
ravines ? "

"Poor fellow!" was all the response the girl
could make; "oh, poor fellow ! And we had so often
wondered together where he came from and where

I came from; and—oh, papa! it is no use trying to look indifferent, I shall miss poor Joe most dreadfully."

"You are not very flattering to me, Mina," said the sheriff, paternally pulling at his silky beard, and standing up at the fireplace. "No doubt I'm an old, useless fellow, but upon my word, it does seem hard that the first hulking rascal who comes about the house should seem so monstrous superior."

"But you know, papa," said Mina, regretting her outburst, "that you encouraged him at first, and brought him here, and praised him, and gave me the idea that in admiring him I was doing what would please you."

"How was I to know, Mina, that the fellow was to turn out such a dead failure? Besides, when I brought him here, along with other men, I freely confess it, I thought he had an income, and I had heard something of substantial expectations, which all turn out to be humbug of the first water. He has no expectations, he has no income. He is only plain Joseph Nixon, of more than doubtful parentage. You know the fair terms, however: he will come back to us when he has found the rest of the deed."

"And he has all the world to find it in," sighed the girl, as the sheriff's man came in to clear the table.

"All the world," said the sheriff, a little sardonically, going out to his study to doze after his cigar was finished, and to waken up to think it time to doze again.

But it was not in Mina's power to take the same easy view of matters. She could not see her lover politely but firmly led to the lodge-gate and have the assurance made to her that he was going out into the world to devote himself to the solution of the enigma of her own birth, without feeling a gratitude which was much allied to pain. While the sheriff was dozing in his study, Mina tossed a cloak across her shoulders: it happened to be one of

white silk which she had worn at a recent opera in
the Edinburgh Theatre Royal; and, thus clad, she
went up into the wooded slope of Corstorphine at
the side of the house. The choice of such a place
at an hour in the evening when the moon was high
in the heavens, was a fair index of the state of her
mind. As she wound out and in among the trees,
the rapidity of her movements showed that every
nerve was strung to its utmost tensity. Presently
she got out into an open space, in the midst of which
there was but one tree-stump. It had often served
her for a resting-place before. She sat down upon
it again, and drew the thin mantle round her, as
she felt the crisp frostiness of the air catch her throat.
The bells of Edinburgh were pealing, tolling, jangling,
striking, with every variety of note and vibration
which, softened by the distance, rolled over the hill
as an invisible wave. Mina had often listened to
them at that height; but to-night there seemed an
undertone of defiant clamour about the pealing

which responded to her own feelings. She looked down over the tree-tops to the road where Nixon must have gone back, and as she sat she could not help asking herself, "Who am I that he should carry a rag of parchment with him to the world's end? How can I be so portentously selfish as to sit down and think of any man doing so much for me? And, poor papa, I think I see through him a little. He has lost faith in the parchment. And he believes in me. And he would like to have me by him always. Oh, how wretched—wretched and weary—I am!"

She was communing with herself in that pessimistic strain, when, from the elms at the further portion of the open space, the sound of footsteps among the twigs became audible. Was it the sheriff who had followed her? For the first time she became aware of the bit of gossamer in which she was clad, knowing how she would be scolded for wandering under a frosty moonlight with nothing more substantial about her. Then a figure appeared, and, as it crossed the space, she saw it was Nixon. It was not possible that he could have watched her coming up the hill, and followed to that old trysting-place. He had bidden her farewell, as she believed, for a very long time. It must be a mere coincidence, and such she soon saw it to be when Nixon, coming within the shadow of the trunk of the tree where she sat, threw up one arm as if in self-defence, and retreated a couple of paces outside the shadow, while he peered into the apparition sitting motionless by itself.

"Joe, it's *me*," said the girl; "I didn't think of your coming back. I fancied there was to be no more of you for a very long time indeed. And I was so vexed with myself that I came over to our old seat in the hollow of the tree-trunk to think I was beside you."

Nixon sat down beside her, and the pair looked out on the large world of white light revealed to them by the shining of the moon.

"I couldn't resist the impulse to return," he said; "but I had no hope of seeing you again. I thought I should like to sit down once more here, and carry away the last impression of your surroundings."

"Joe," replied the girl, "I have been thinking that I should like to release you from—from—I have no right, dear, to allow you to accept a mission like that imposed upon you by the sheriff. He is pleased, poor papa, to do anything that shall keep you at a distance. Now, I don't like it; I won't have it. I shall have no good man running a wild-goose chase for me. It is all a mystery about me. Let it remain a mystery. And, after all, there is nothing in these scraps of parchment that might not refer to any one else. Joe, dear, give it up; and set your mind to something else."

Nixon had not given serious thought to the impracticable nature of the quest since he bade her good-bye earlier in the evening. He was so overwhelmed by the sense of separation that the new departure had not begun to loom before him. It did so now, however, and with all the impassioned gallantry of his love on him, he replied,—

"But, Mina, there must be some solution to the mystery. You must have been born somewhere. Somebody must have been your father, and some other body must have been your mother. And *your* mother and father must have been known to quite a host of people. To tell the truth, Mina, I rather think the good sheriff has never cared to make his inquiries too profound, never caring to lose you. But I shall be very thorough, starting as I do with the conviction that a mother you must have had, and a father you must have had."

"Why, Joe, of course; that is not much of a discovery; we knew that years and years ago. That has been assumed by everybody who has looked at the parchment."

"Yes, no doubt; but what has it led to? In my case it will lead to something of importance, for I shall find a chip of the ship in which you were wrecked when the sheriff had you first put into his arms; I shall find an expert who shall tell me what the wood is, and in what part of the world they build with it. I shall follow up that clue to the dockyard, and from thence I shall branch out into the ship's history—who her captains were, if I have found her name; or it may be that half a dozen, or half a score, built of the same material, launched on the same seas and wrecked about the same time, may have to be traced. Well, I will trace them all, arrive at their passenger lists, and, it may be, in the course of time, get a hint of how you came to be on board."

"Oh, you silly old Joe," said Mina, leaning her head upon his shoulder, and accepting the pressure of her hands within his own. "By that time you will have met twenty girls prettier—am I pretty, Joe?—and better than I am, and there will be grey hairs in your head, and I shall be a melancholy old spinster. Find some other way."

They sat looking out upon the descending glades until a wreath of mist began to crawl among the lower trees, when Mina, with a little shiver, rose and said she had been too long away; she would be missed, and the sheriff would be anxious. Nixon stood up also, but before they parted he had replied,—

"Mina, you think it too much of me to give some years of my life to this pursuit. I do not think it too much. In any event I have to leave Edinburgh to find a livelihood. The search for bread can go hand in hand with this search. I am as likely to find it in one place as in another. Once more— only promise me, Mina, not to be impatient."

"Joseph, I will wait," were the last words he heard, as her figure disappeared among the dark trees.

CHAPTER V.

AN OLD COACH ROAD.

STANDING among the statues of the Parliament House, half a dozen of the briefless ones discussed Nixon's failure and disheartenment, and determined to give him a little supper. It was known of Nixon that when he said anything he always meant it, and having declared his intention of no more putting his wig to his head or his gown to his back, the fact was accepted as final.

"What will Joseph do?" one and another of them asked.

"Put on a red coat and learn the goose step," suggested an admirer of his muscle.

"Go abroad," said another, vaguely thinking of

the vague region to which so many of the baffled turn. But none of the conjectures were satisfactory; all they knew was] that Joseph would go away, and that before he went they cared to wish him God-speed. While they talked of him, Usher went sweeping past, a volume of precedents in his hand, carrying his head very .high in the air. " M'lud," cried a briefless one, " we're going to give Nixon a supper at the Rainbow. Will your ludship so far condescend as to take the chair ? "

Usher stopped, *en route* for the great library of the advocates, turned in among the unemployed, and, with an air of instructed affability, declared that nothing in the world would give him more pleasure. At what hour did they propose to sup ? And what lengths did they intend to go in the matter of viands ? Yes, let him alone just now, and he would join them in the evening. In the evening, therefore, Joseph went up from his lodgings to the North Bridge, and found a dozen of his male friends waiting him in a private room, which presently warmed up with the mists of a mighty haggis, above which Usher, with reverent eyes, stretched his hand, mumbling, "Weel, are ye worthy o' a grace, and lang's my airm, amen?" The guest of the evening did not look so cheery as the chairman. He was visibly trying to pluck up his spirits and to put a hopeful face upon his difficulties ; but a man may not lose his profession and suffer impending banishment from his sweetheart without a little uneasiness. Still, to a northern constitution, there is something irresistible about the ancient haggis. And, on this occasion, Usher accompanied his distribution of the plates with so much apt rhetoric and quotation that even Joseph's long-drawn countenance relaxed as he was invited to witness "the dews distil like amber bead." In a short time he was adding his laugh to the shouts of laughter when Usher went over his thirteen imitations of the thirteen judges of the Inner and Outer Houses. Nor did the hilarity raised by that rapid presentation of the senators the least interfere with the quality of Usher's pathos when he came to the speech in which he characterized Nixon as a companion, a friend, and a man.

"I did not know Joseph in his cradle," he said, remembering full well that who rocked that cradle was as little known to Joseph as to himself, "but I knew him when he was a 'gyte' in the High School and when he was beginning to exercise a potent toe upon the football of the yard. He will not misunderstand me when I add that the promise he gave in his kicking boyhood has hardly been fulfilled. In his manhood he declines to kick. Rather than kick, he prefers to withdraw from the glorious combatancy of the bar, in order that he may lead his own life. I think he is wrong. I consider him to be impatient. I think if he would wait, he might still match his voice with those thirteen voices I have humbly attempted to illustrate, with their peculiarities of accent and intonation. But since he will not renew and prolong his patience, we must offer him, one and all, the tribute of our affectionate admiration. We know why he will not stay. His heart is too large. If I said it beat like a sledge-hammer I should be within the mark. Joseph Nixon has the giant's strength, as we who have seen him run, swim, and wrestle, know full well, but he declines to use it as a giant. He goes, however, to a combat where that strength will serve him well. No more than you do I know where he is to establish himself for the fight. We will not push our inquiries to the verge of impertinence and ask him, since he wishes to keep it a secret. What we know, however, is that whether he be on the prairies of America, the steppes of Russia, the bush of Australia, or the plantations of India, he will carry with him the good-will, the affection, and the regret of his friends of Parliament House. Charge your glasses, and drink deep."

So spoke Usher, and Nixon standing up to respond,

as he looked through the steam of toddy and the reek of the pipes, and saw a dozen sorrowful, hard, friendly faces looking at him, was as unable to find an expression for his feelings as he was the other day in the Outer House to argue a little brief. All he could get out was, "I thank you from the bottom of my heart," after which he sat down, and made himself as noisy in conversation as he could, to compensate for the lack of consecutive speech when he was on his legs. The evening passed rapidly away, and when Usher, putting his arm inside Nixon's, pulled him from the effusive hand-shaking of the mellow dozen, and strolled with him round the Castle from the top of the High Street, it was long past midnight. In that last half hour, however, the cool-headed chairman got everything out of his friend that he wanted.

"Your first plan is, my boy?" asked Usher, as beneath the shadow of the overhanging rock, they saw the moonlight discovering every cranny of the

Grass Market. "Your first plan is?"

"To try for gold."

"Very good, and are you going straight out to Australia, or are you to try our own new field first?"

"To-morrow I set out for Cnoc Dhu. I see nuggets have been found half an ounce in weight, in the valley of the Rudder."

"Doesn't it seem a waste of time?"

"In any case, I would go there first. I have to find out what I can about Mina. Gold or no, the beginning of my search must date from that district."

The pair emerged from the shadow of the Castle, Usher silent for a time, still having his arm linked to Nixon's.

"What," he asked abruptly, "does Miss Durie want with a new parentage? Hasn't the Sheriff taken her up? And isn't it a well-known fact—I know the man who drew his will—that she is his heir to the utmost farthing he possesses, and the

Sheriff has a pretty competence to leave behind him. He doesn't often mention it; but it's the fact that he had an old uncle in the oil trade who passed over two-thirds of his earnings to him, and that greasy industry is, I may say, a very lucrative one indeed."

· " Mina wants to know who her father and mother were."

"And you will allow that bit of curiosity to come between you and your fortune, my poor Quixote— here we are at your own door. I will be at the Aberdeen train to-morrow morning."

True to his word, Usher went to the railway station and shook hands, at a third-class carriage, with his friend.

" You certainly couldn't be pronounced a member of our faculty, Joe," said he, peering in at Nixon, who, clad in a coarse serge jacket and common striped trousers, looked like the mate of a timber ship going off to join her at some northern port. "What luggage have you ? "

" A patent india-rubber canoe in the guard's van."

" You are an impracticable rascal. You can't dig with a canoe. I should have thought a selection of shovels would have suited you better. Here's one of the Sappers and Miners in full uniform. Put out your head and look at him. Now, if you could get him to effect an exchange with you, that's the sort of thing that would help you to fill your pockets with nuggets. But, by the way, have you seen the papers this morning? No? I must get you one."

He went to a bookstall and bought a paper, un-folded it, and pointed to a paragraph about the diggings at Cnoc Dhu.

" I was going to say you are not such a fool as you look, Joe; for there is an account of an urchin, with a tin pannikin, washing five pounds' worth of gold out of the shingle at the foot of his father's garden. Some of the '51 miners have already arrived at Ruddersdale, and the inhabitants of the moun-tains are wild with emotion. Whew! the train's off.

Good-bye, old fellow; good-bye. Luck be with you, and when you come into your kingdom remember me with briefs."

The train snorted out of the station, and the friends parted, Nixon's eyes dim with emotion as he thrust himself in a corner of his carriage and looked ruefully at his portmanteau. Travel, however, even the mild variety of it which consists of getting into a carriage at one station and getting out at another more or less remote, has a healthful and awakening effect. He was not twenty miles on his road north before he was diplomatizing with a Presbyterian clergyman who had joined him as to whether he might not smoke with his head out of the window. Then the minister went out and two sailors came in, and he found himself taken for one of their profession, and was obliged to trot out all the knowledge of ships he possessed to keep himself in countenance with his company. By-and-by they got out, and a couple of farmers and a draper came

in, and he was taken for a "commercial gentleman"
in a small way, and talked to accordingly—each
incident, very little stirring in itself, but sufficiently
so to keep him in conversational relations with his
neighbours. At Aberdeen he stayed an evening at
a small coffee-house near the quay, and next day
went round by sea to the outermost edge of the
Marnock Firth. From thence, having reached the
limits of the railway system, he took a place on
a stage coach which passed Ruddersdale on its
way to the extremity of the island. Every ten miles
the coach stopped at a village or hamlet, and had
fresh horses put in. Nixon found this kind of
locomotion very agreeable. He sat on the top, with
his canoe at his feet and his portmanteau strapped
in position in front of him. The driver was rather
a taciturn, self-contained man, not inclined to speak
much, perhaps because the north wind rushed down
his throat and deprived him of the advantages of
his last glass of grog when he did speak, or perhaps

because of his high sense of responsibility at the reins. The guard, however, who sat perched upon a little chair of iron above and behind the coach, spoke freely when he was not awakening the echoes of a village with his horn. Nixon's spirits rose at the sight of the mountains which began to loom into view in the horizon. There was Cnoc This and Ben That clustered together, and the guard named them all and told their heights as if they were members of his own family who had visibly grown under maternal feeding. Then, quite suddenly, the road was overhung with forest, and they saw them no more, though the Firth spread to the right of them, sending its white waves among the boulders below. Every turn in the road now opened up a new scene of beauty, either a bridge over a stream with boats lying at anchor, or a stretch of golden sand, with the red-legs wading at the verge of the sea, or a "shaw" of sheltered ash, smelling of spring, and resounding with the shrill screech of the wren and the chaffinch. A stage before they came to Ruddersdale, at a little straw-thatched clachan, they were joined by a small grey-haired man, firmly knit, with a serious red face, in which a pair of small eyes looked piercingly above a massive Roman nose. His greyness was not that of old age, but rather the hue of a man who had roughed it in different climates since his youth. He passed up to the top of the coach just such a collection of objects as Usher had pointed out in the hands of the sapper. "Mind my cradle now; do," he shouted, as the coachman took a box out of his hands. "It has got to dandle the little darlings over there," pointing towards the "airt" in which Cnoc Dhu lay.

"You're going to dig, are you?" asked Nixon, making room for him on his seat.

"Well, I'm thinking about it," said the stranger, "I've been wakened up from five years' sleep in my little cottage at the other side of the Firth, by all these reports. My wife, she says I'll catch my death of rheumatism, but I say better die of rheumatism than die of the unsatisfied gold fever. Is there anything new, Mr. Laggan, from the field ?"

"For the diggings, gentlemen ?" asked the guard cheerily, blowing into his tin trumpet and dropping a bag into the arms of a man who came out from a roadside house. "News! you will find when you get as far as Ruddersdale that they can talk nothing but gold, and that's news enough. I haven't seen the colour of much of it myself, but they believe in it. Why, the schoolmaster hasn't had a boy in his school since the rumour first went out. They are all turning over stones from morning to night on the beach—more crabs than gold there," and the guard again addressed himself to his horn. "On the hill, gentlemen, behind Ruddersdale, the entire clan Mackay may be seen any day, glowering at the entire clan Gun, on the other hill beyond the Rudder, and there *they* are pickaxing, delving, draining. They've reclaimed a moor already, though. It's what they wouldn't do under any other provocation."

"But, surely," said the stranger, "there's some better work than that going on. I've been in five-and-twenty Victoria creeks in my time, and crushed as much quartz as any digger of them all on the other side of the line, but I never heard of a couple of clans being allowed to go bald-headed to their work like that. Surely, you have a proprietor and a permit-office, and some way of getting along."

"There's Leslie, the banker," said the guard. "If they do get any gold, it goes into his office."

"Who owns the Rudder?" asked Nixon.

"Ah, that's the question," said the guard. "Who, indeed! I say Leslie owns it now. At any rate, he might as well own it as hold it. There's a pair of them would like to own it—a duke on this side of the water, and a duke on the other side of the water, who would give any money for it, and the land on its banks, and Cnoc Dhu, and the mountains at the source of it. That they would. But it's on the way to the Crown, they say. For Sir Thomas Dunbeath—he was a peculiar, half-cracked gentleman, who wouldn't stay at home at any time—he's disappeared these, let me see, these fifteen, sixteen, aye, these eighteen years, and he was the last of his race. Leslie, he administers the estate for the Courts of Session, and if Sir Thomas don't look sharp about it, he'll be administering it for the Crown. It's a fine property in its way, and a pity that the fat of it should go into Leslie's hands. That's what I say—a man with no more conscience than a herring."

"Are you going to dig?" asked the stranger, abruptly, turning to Nixon.

"I am."

"Have you ever dug before?"

"No."

"All right. I want a chum. Will we try our luck together?"

"I don't mind if we do," said Nixon; and the coach rolled over the bridge and into Ruddersdale.

CHAPTER VI.

USHER'S TEMPTATION.

FRANK USHER looked regretfully over the North
Bridge in the direction of the train in which his
friend had set out on his search for fortune. He
was sorry all the way up to Parliament House, and
he was even a little sorry inside the House, when
he was hoisting himself into his gown and telling
a neighbour, similarly engaged, that Joseph had
departed. At the same time his distress was mingled
with a little contempt. He regarded the withdrawal
from the bar as an act of simple cowardice, and he
was piqued to think that now Joseph was gone there
was no serious rival he need fear in his approaches
to Mina Durie. Usher's nature was one which set

small value on the attainment of anything which was not surrounded with difficulty. So far as he had gone, he had only experienced difficulties to overcome them. At a bar where there were not a great many yearly thousands to distribute among a good many competing hundreds, he had contrived to make a fair stand, and to let his voice be heard when companions who had started with him were dawdling and waiting for the day which never came. His early success, though it was only genteel poverty as yet, had given him rather a truculent point of view from which to regard things in general. The world, he felt, was made for him, and its good things all lying in wait for his enjoyment. He was willing to slowly work his way to the position in which he thought he could have and hold the prize; for he had unbounded confidence in himself, justified by the effect some of his dashing speeches had already produced upon juries. It was a sign of his self-assurance that he had gone into a house and furnished it, and begun to dispense hospitalities which as yet he was unable to pay for. His father, being a Custom House officer on some remote coast, was not able to send him the monthly cheque on which so many of his intimate friends survived. But though he had begun to live beyond his means, he had the appearance of success written on his face, and his tradespeople were not anxious. He was not the least anxious himself, but showed the dashing front and slightly loud demeanour of a man who was rising, who meant to rise, and who had no doubts about his ultimate elevation. It had been an immense surprise to him when, some months before, it was whispered about that Mina Durie and Joseph Nixon were engaged. He had been in the habit of seeing a good deal of the sheriff's ward at Durie Den and in houses in town. He knew that she cared for Joseph, but he thought it was in the same way as he cared—with a kind of affectionate patronage, as if he were a mastiff or a retriever, who might be petted or snubbed without reference to his feelings. So secure had he been in his own sense of possession of the girl that he had been in no great hurry to tell her how often he pictured her to himself as the mistress of his household; he had gone on thinking of Joseph as the mastiff, and lo! the dog had served him a trick which he saw no present way of turning to that animal's disadvantage. At all events, Joseph being gone to the diggings, he was in a favourable position for turning the situation. Mina should see a good deal of him now; the sheriff was his very good friend; anything might happen to reverse the decision of a premature flirtation. Usher's house, midway between the east and west end of Edinburgh, was visited the same evening by a hale, genteel man of middle age, who was shown into the crowded study of the advocate.

"Ah, Porteous, how d'ye do?" said the advocate rising from his desk; "I hope you're bringing grist to the mill. How can I advise you? What is it?"

The visitor was a stock-broker, and had the air of subdued opulence which belongs to a man, not himself rich, but dealing with the material out of which riches are created. Mr. Porteous was not one of the tribe of fussy plungers who swallow up the earnings of the injudicious middle-classes; he operated for the most part with the surplus of retired officers, Indian civilians, old ladies, and such like, and had the reputation of being a safe and prudent man, who rarely made losses. Usher was glad to see him in his study; for his financial clients belonged to a class who, to relieve the tedium of existence, often quarrelled and brought their quarrels into court, whence came briefs.

"What do you think o' that?" asked the stock-broker without further ado, taking from his waistcoat pocket a small pareel and unfolding it.

Usher looked into the tissue-paper which, inside a cotton rag, contained a handful of yellow grains.

"Is it a retainer, Porteous? Guineas in the raw? Let me hear all about it."

Porteous handed him a letter in reply to his query, and Usher read :—

"There is no doubt about the existence of gold in the valley of the Rudder. The question is, in what quantities may we expect to find it? The accompanying parcel of gold was brought to me by one of my own shepherds from Cnoc Dhu, whose daughter washed it out of a brook at the side of their shieling. I did my best to keep the discovery from being noised abroad, but I was foolish enough to give the man a sovereign for the dust he brought me." ("I should say," murmured Usher, "that the man had very decidedly the worst of the bargain.") "He showed the sovereign to his daughter, and she told an old woman who keeps a small 'howff,' and in a few days the whole neighbourhood was out about, digging and hammering. I cannot say that they have been successful in obtaining gold. And I have to add that a skilled geologist, who has read papers before the British Association, dined with me the other day, and he gives it as his opinion, formed upon an intimate acquaintanceship with the formation of the rocks of the valley of the Rudder, that gold can only occur in what he calls 'infinitesimal quantities.' Still he is only a geologist and not a practical man, and his opinion need not be accepted as final. There may be more gold than he supposes, and, at all events, there is certainly enough for the purpose which I entertain in connection with it. As you are aware, the lands of Ruddersdale, from Cnoc Dhu to the sea, may soon pass from my control. They may be administered by some one vested at the Parliament House, working for the Crown. I consider myself very shabbily treated, with that contingency held up before me, and I believe that the present is an opportunity fairly presented to me in which I may recoup myself for many arduous services, never likely to be otherwise rewarded. And what I propose to you, my friend, is this. Whether there be gold on the Rudder or not, there is the reputation of gold, which in your way of life is as good. Now I have it in my power to allot ground for digging and sinking shafts either to individuals or to a company, and if you can make up a small directorate and get the enterprise launched upon the Exchange, we will find as much gold as will satisfy any reasonable body of shareholders for a few months." ("For a few months," murmured Usher, scrutinizing his friend keenly. "That is very delicate. A good man, Mr. Leslie. An admirable, good man.") "When the supply of gold comes to an end the power of working the mine will have passed to some other body."

"And that is the great Leslie's opinion of his duty in the present emergency of a discovery of gold," said Usher. "How do you know," he asked abruptly, "that this stuff ever came out of the Rudder at all ? He is evidently prepared to go great lengths for his company."

"Here is a paper published up in those regions. It gives a full account of an interview with the shepherd

—a plain, unvarnished tale, Usher. There is no doubt about the precious metal. I believe in it, and I mean to have it on 'Change."

"Then you have a faith in the simple credulity of your countrymen which history and experience have not taught me to expect. You may as well promise them diamonds. You couldn't draw a prospectus that wouldn't glitter so confoundedly that every investor north of the Tweed would be pelting it with proverbs as he proceeded to button up his breeches pocket."

"This is an international age."

"You are becoming profound, Porteous. What are you driving at?"

"There are investors beyond the Tweed and Exchanges out of the empire. I am looking ahead. This precious mine may not be to the mind of our countrymen. Very well, there is the Bourse in Paris, and a great deal of romantic expectation always hovering about it. If we can't get our mine to go in our own Exchanges we shall carry it to Paris. You begin to see why I have called on you."

"Not as yet, unless it is that you mean to allot me the law business of the company when it is started. Judging from the tone and intention of this letter, I should say that there is likely to be a good deal of law wanted. And," he added slowly, "I think the man who acts for the other side will have the best cause to plead."

CHAPTER VII.

A LITTLE OBTUSE.

"You are rather hasty about it," said Porteous after a pause. "You know I have a reputation to keep up for safety and solidity. Now, I can't afford to put a 'salted' mine on the market, if that is what you suspect. I have rather overdone my caution, however, and find that I am getting voted slow and old-fashioned. I can stand this gold-mine episode, therefore, even if it don't turn out El Dorado. Now, my dear sir, draw us out a nice, catching prospectus— a something that will appeal to sensible men, you understand—holding out moderate prospects of dividend. Let there be no blarney in it, but make it, as you know very well how—make it an attractive statement of the prospects of the company, based upon the finds of gold already made. You may announce that a thousand pounds' worth of gold has been washed out of the alluvium of the Rudder before the prospectus has been issued. Here is a chart of the locality. That's the lie of the river and the land; there are the mountains. Shafts may be sunk anywhere between Ruddersdale and Cnoc Dhu."

"But in a short time this will become Crown property, if Sir Thomas Dunbeath doesn't make his appearance. It seems to me Leslie will only hurry up his own dismissal, if there really be gold. It looks like putting a hand on the regalia."

"It would if the Company didn't pay the estate well for working its supposititious minerals. But the right will be well paid for, and can be regarded as rent just as much as one of the sheep-farms."

"Well?"

"You are a little obtuse, Usher, for so sharp a man.

What are you waiting for ? What are you balancing in your mind ? "

"I have not done this sort of work before. It goes a little against the grain. I shall be a judge one day, and there must be no blot on my escutcheon. Perhaps I have no very large admiration for virtue in the abstract. It's inconvenient to a man of taste. Its laws rasp the ancles and the wrists like the gyves of a gaoler. But virtue in my line is a mode of promotion, and I must hesitate before I put my hand to anything which might serve to compromise me."

"I have a reputation, too, I hope," said Porteous, testily, "and what would inconvenience you would ruin me. My dear sir, if you have any question of conscience, I need only put these proposals in my pocket and carry them across the street to you know who ? I hope his reputation is up to the mark."

"Stop ; don't be in such a hurry. Lay down your

chart of the district, and give me a day or two to decide over this business. I mustn't put in too many nuggets I suppose," he added, shaking hands with his visitor at the door.

CHAPTER VIII.

As the mail-coach drew up at the Duke's Arms, Ruddersdale, Nixon's long-nosed friend handed down his cradle and his baggage and waited.

"We don't go in here," he said, looking defiantly at a stout inn-keeper, wearing a white hat, who seemed to expect a visit from them. "Men who come to dig can't afford that style. Dear beds, dear mutton, dear liquor, and a shedding of shillings that would soon leave our purses—mine, anyhow—as empty as a last year's swallow's nest."

"And mine, too," said Nixon, standing over his rubber canoe and his portmanteau. "I think there must be something nearer our style along the shore."

Mr. Laggan, the guard, came round on them for the shillings which were not included in the fare, and whispered that there was a Nancy Harper's, about a couple of hundred yards off the square; not a great house, by any means, but clean and tidy, and moderate. If they went out of the square at the corner of Mr. Leslie's bank, down by the thatches, they would see Nancy's sign swinging in the wind, "and just mention, quietly, that he, Mr. Laggan, had sent them."

" Here, lad ! " called out the stranger, to a boy with a barrow, "lift in these shovels, and that box, and that, and that, and that, and go down the square, at the corner of the bank, to Nancy Harper's."

The coach drove into a yard behind the Duke's Arms. The landlord stood with an expression of contempt on his face as he saw the direction the baggage of the pair was taking, and from an upper window looking on the square, some highly-flushed faces appeared on the scene, amidst laughter, and a voice called out—

" New chums, by Jove ! "

" There's an old digger up there," said Nixon's new friend, as the barrow, preceding them, passed the corner of the bank, and made for the swinging sign of Nancy Harper.

Nancy had not expected anybody by the coach, for she was not at her white-washed step watching. She had to be called out from her bar, a little room with a mysterious door, and a slit of a window looking out upon a well-darkened passage. She did the honours of reception very well, however, when she made her appearance, and she smiled benevolently when she was told that her visitors had come to the diggings.

" Weel, weel ! " said Nancy, showing them into her coffee-room, which was a spacious kitchen, with a stone floor and a vast fire blazing on the hearth; " ye micht be doin' waur than trying your luck. But I'm no for believin' in the goold myself. It wadna have been lying there a' this time—we're unco' fond o' the goold in Ruddersdale, and there's been guid een at

Cnoc Dhu ere ever Oliver Gun and his wife and Elspeth began lookin' at the burns. Truly, gentlemen, if you'll believe me, you'll take your spades to my back-garden and dig for worms, and get two or three dizzen red-trout to yourselves; it'll pay you better, and the work's not so hard."

" What do *you* think ? " asked the stranger of a bowed man, leaning, with a shawl about him, towards the hearth.

" He's deef," said Nancy ; " he's asking you what do you think about the goold ? "

" Filthy lucre ! " said the old man, wiping his parched lips with his tongue, and looking with watery eyes towards a bottle which Nancy laid on the table ; " the root of all evil."

" You keep your own moralist, Mrs. Harper," observed Nixon.

" I keep my feyther ! " she said abruptly, removing half-a-dozen chops from the fire and tumbling them precipitately upon an " ashet." " Now fa' to, and if ye maun dig, gang at it wi' something in your insides. I've nae doot, if ye tak' your spades to the sea-shore you'll get a bit hole to yourselves, and nobody will interfere wi' you. It'll do ye good, maybe; there's a braw fine wind comes in from the Firth. Coming—coming."

And Nancy disappeared to the slit in the wall, where she was being solicited for drams by some fishermen from the shore.

"She's a shrewd woman," said the stranger; "but, I say, if we're going to chum, it's about time we exchanged cards. What's your name?"

"I didn't think of that," said Nixon. "What would you advise? What would be a good mining name?"

The stranger looked suspiciously at him, as if he were suddenly revealed as an escaped convict.

"Well, I've mined extensively, as I've told you, beneath the Southern Cross, at many different points and among numerous different companies: but I've always mined as the same man. I'm not ashamed to be myself. I thought from the colour of your eyes, and the expression of your face, that neither would you. I am John Russell, miner."

"And I am Joseph Nixon, miner also."

"Very good then, Nixon. Let's light up, and see what is to be seen."

"And heard," said Nixon, lifting a bit of hot peat in the tongs and applying it to the bowl of his pipe. They had not far to go to the shore. The basin of the harbour opened at their feet, and herring-boats rocked their masts towards each other, as the heave of the sea insinuated itself from without. On the quay there was nothing more enlivening to be seen than a few creels and barrels; but from the end of it they saw up Ruddersdale to the overhanging forest of ashes and firs, and heard the bell toll in the steeple at the head of the square, and watched the starlings wheel round it. The shore-line beyond Ruddersdale was visible, too, whitened by surf all the way to the mountainous precipices of Cnoc; and it was a relief to turn from them to the quiet meandering of the Rudder, issuing slow and deep from beneath its bridge to join the deep sea. Nixon leant, very silent, on the keel of an upturned boat and looked dreamily over the sea. He had done, in his time, a good deal of manual labour; but it was of that description which falls under the head of amusement. He had rowed, wrestled, shot, fished, golfed, run, and boxed—all forms of hard work ; but it had only been in response to the call of his muscular system. He had not needed to work. Now, however, he was face to face with necessity, and the compulsion which was sending him to handle the spade and the pickaxe saddened him a little. His new friend was looking into all the mysteries of the quay, and exchanging sentiments with a sou'-wester which showed itself aft of a herring-boat. The sou'-wester was sceptical about gold. His lads had got none, anyhow. He knew only of about five pounds worth being got altogether.

He was a deep man, Mr. Leslie. Nixon heard him utter these remarks, and the desolation of his own circumstances seemed to stand out clear before him in the light of them. What if he dug and failed? He could not return to Sheriff Durie and say to him:

"I have done my best. I have tried to fill my pockets so as to hold out in my search for Mina's father. But there has been no treasure for me in the valley of the Rudder. I have found nothing. I have learnt nothing. Now, give me Mina."

"Nixon," said Russell, returning from his conversation, "they don't much believe in it, the old ones. Suppose we go up the river a bit and form a judgment. I rather think I can spot a rich patch with any man. As yet there are few knowing hands arrived. They won't be long, though. If they have the fever in their veins as I begin to experience it, they will be down here in hundreds."

"I'll go back for my canoe."

"And in the meantime I shall interview Leslie. Meet me at the bridge."

Nixon got his canoe and stood with it at the bridge for the better part of an hour. Then, Russell showing no sign of appearing, he went down and launched himself into the centre of the stream. There was something of the Indian in him, he felt, as he threw aside the water with his paddle and shot up the Rudder. Above the bridge there was a low range of blasted rocks, from which the stones of the town had probably been taken when it was built. The water rushed through them deep and rapid, but he soon pushed his canoe through the stone gate and got behind the town, where the ridges of the river were brown with heath. He saw some of the good people digging, exactly as they might have searched for worms, and they stopped to shade their eyes, and look at him as he sped rapidly by. Some of the bow-legged little boys tossed their caps in the air and cheered him. It was evident that they regarded him as part of the new world of wonder opened up in these recent weeks by the rumour of gold. On the water Nixon recovered his spirits with the use of his arm. The lost sense of personal power came back to him, and as he drove up rapids and circled whirlpools and crossed tranquil long pools, the inward vista of mountains becoming clear to his eye, he thoroughly recovered himself. There might indeed be no gold beyond these waters, but what a heaven hung over them! what a joyous bleating of young lambs was going on beside them! what a calling of bird to bird flying on the wing! The further he paddled, however, the more frequently he passed long strands of shingle and sand, strands where the sand-pipers were calling just now, but where as yet no digger had inserted an experimental spade. On the whole, he considered there was some hope, and he returned late to Nancy Harper's with a hopeful expression on his face.

"Weel, sir," inquired that grey dame, "have you

no' a nieve fu' o' siller ta give me? No? An' you so far up the Rudder as that!—I canna' believe ye, when ye tell me ye got ten miles up. Ye would see Cnoc Dhu; was there any mist on it's top? Sirs, I'll give ye a kipper to your supper. Mr. Russell's ta'en a room upstairs. He's there if ye want to find him."

Nixon went upstairs and found his friend in his shirt-sleeves, scouring a perforated sheet of iron in the end of his cradle. His implements were all un-loosened, and picks and shovels lay about the floor. He looked up rather doubtfully from his work as Joseph entered, and made a poor effort to talk with his pipe between his teeth.

"I've had the big man here," he said, "and he's been good enough to inspect all my mining material."

"You mean Leslie?"

"Yes, and he's made me a proposal. He believes in the gold, and he's going to work the stream with a company. He says what I believe is very true, that in the course of a few weeks, Ruddersdale will be full of skilled miners. Well, he wants me to pick them as they come in, and begin sinking shafts, and he'll pay us fair wages. What d'ye think?"

"I'll work for wages if it must be ; but I'd rather dig on my own account."

"Nixon, I'm obliged to say it to you; but if Joseph Nixon be your name, it's a misfortune to you. What have you done? Don't mind me. I know all sorts. I've herded with cut-throats and cut-purses, and know enough of life to know that they aren't the worst kind of fellows. What have you done to make an old lawyer like Leslie put his hand to his brow when I mention the name of Joseph Nixon, and ask for leave for him to riddle the waste dirt between this and Cnoc Dhu—put his hand to his brow, and look as if he were going off in a dead faint? The apparition of the devil couldn't have disturbed the man more than the name of Joseph Nixon. You had some reason, then, for concealing your real name?"

"I know nothing of him, except what we heard from the guard. It could hardly be my name that made him squeamish."

"It was, though; and he stood up against that mantelpiece, the beads of perspiration coming out of his brow, and his jaws getting jaundiced with terror. 'What is this Nixon you want a permit for?' he asked, when he had recovered the use of his voice. 'Is he a lawyer?' To which I replied, feeling very sure that I was in the right for once. 'No, he's no lawyer; he's just a very good fellow, who has come along with me to dig for gold.' So there's your permit, Nixon, and you may thank me for getting it."

"I don't understand it," said Nixon. "I am, or rather was, a lawyer. But I never had dealings with Leslie. Are you perfectly sure it was my name which affected him?"

"Then there's some mystery about you, after all! I thought your hands were deuced unlike a miner's. I'm as sure as I am of my own cradle that when

Leslie signed that permit, and wrote the name of Joseph Nixon, he trembled from top to toe. Look at the writing yourself."

"Oh, writing's no test of anything. I've seen the coolest hands sprawl, and the most nervous ones write copper-plate. It's only a trick of the muscles of the fingers, and isn't connected with a man's nature at all."

"Perhaps he's a relation of yours," said the miner, polishing the rust off the face of a spade.

"I have no relations," said Nixon, painfully.

"That's too good to be true. I never heard of a man so pleasantly situated."

"If you had my experience you wouldn't think so."

"Well, you may take my word for it that this Leslie hasn't heard of you for the first time."

Nixon was silent for a long time; then he took off his coat and helped his friend at his scouring.

CHAPTER IX.

GOLFING.

" MINA is visiting at Merchiston, Usher, this afternoon. If you have nothing better to do you might
come round the Bruntsfield Links with me in a
friendly match. The ground should be in excellent
condition; there has been a high, dry north wind
blowing over it for the last three days. I feel in a
mood for handling the club and the cleek. She
knows I am going over the course, and will probably
join us in the afternoon. Afterwards you might
drive round with us and dine."

So spoke Sheriff Durie to advocate Usher in the
hall of justice, and the latter being only too anxious
to see Mina Durie, and the aspect she presented in

the absence of Nixon, closed with the proposal at once.

"Thank you, sheriff; there is no particular reason why I should be here any more than on the Bruntsfield Links. My work is done; but though I know I shall only match my club against yours to get a licking, I shall do my best."

"I'm not so sure about the licking, Usher. Certainly, I have the advantage of you in long practice, but to-day we start so far equal, that neither of us has had a club in hand all winter."

There was no one on the links when the pair reached the green upland, except a few servant-maids in a corner beating carpets.

"I suppose your clubs are in the club-house," said the sheriff.

"I play with Nixon's set," said Usher. "He had them specially made for himself, if you remember. He had strong views about the shaft of his club, and wouldn't touch a ball with hickory to save his life

He had no belief in hickory, and I defy any one to say what sort of wood he had put into them."

"You are playing Nixon's game in his absence?" inquired the sheriff, with the faintest accent of suspicion, and with a decided diminution of cordiality in his tone.

"My own game, with Nixon's clubs."

"Ah! very good; I daresay we shall find a couple of caddies outside to carry our things."

They found half a score of "caddies" only too willing to go round the links with them, and with the undiminished north wind still sweeping across the field, they started for the first hole, the sheriff looking very determined and sportsmanlike in his red coat, Usher, not equipped in the same way, feeling rather nervous at his approaching meeting with Mina. To the sheriff, golf was one of the choicest delights in life. It was one of the things he could do thoroughly well. He rarely met an opponent on any breadth of downs who could come near him in holing. It was one of the consolations he had for being a decidedly poor judge, for it must be said of him, in his official capacity, that he held his place in virtue of being a very gentlemanly man, agreeably known to the influential persons who made such appointments as his. Everybody knew that his substitute in the remote county of which he had the jurisdiction, understood law a great deal better than himself; but they also knew that Sheriff Durie had a lively conviction of that fact, on which circumstance there was a guarantee for the course of justice running smoothly.

"I daresay," said the sheriff, the wind blowing his silky beard about his face, "Mina will see us from the window of the house she has called at. Ah! yes; there she is, waving her hand. You see her? I say to be sure, what a furious blast of wind! Phew! How your hat spins along!"

The wind had indeed lifted Usher's hat, and blown it as high as a respectable kite might ascend, and it was at that moment bowling it along the links at the rate of ten miles an hour. Half-a-dozen caddies set out after it; Mina and her friends crowded to their window to see the eccentric behaviour of it. Usher stood, with a vacant expression of amused geniality on his face, until the hat was restored; then the sheriff, having "tee'd" his ball, stretched himself, looked into the distance, shouted "'fore" to a man with a basket on his head, who stood in the way to examine him, hit off with a resounding whack, and the game began. The white ball went high in the air, and Usher looking at it said :—

"Well, for the first drive of the year, sheriff, I call that magnificent!"

"It's pretty fair, I think," said the sheriff, inwardly wishing that there had been more spectators than the caddies to see how it was done. Usher then tee'd his ball, raised his club, but instead of lifting it into the air, he threw up a cloud of turf round it, the ball awkwardly rolling off to a neighbouring sandhole.

"Give me hickory," cried the sheriff, walking away

with his admiring caddy behind him, as he left Usher to fish up his ball with a cleek, the party in the window looking on with apparent delight at the advocate's confusion. He was still labouring away at the bunker when his opponent had holed his ball down the links. He was dismally engaged there when Mina Durie rejoined him.

"You have been very unfortunate," said the sheriff's ward, "just at the outset to find yourself in a bunker. Papa always has all the luck on his side, and beats everybody. It was bold of you, wasn't it, to accept his challenge ?"

"It would have been, if I had been fool enough to think myself a match for him," said Usher, throwing up his ball, with a plentiful accompaniment of sand, and following it for a stroke in the direction of the sheriff.

Mina's feet and ankles were uncovered by the blast, and Usher could not help noticing how prettily moulded they were. The girl seemed to be aware that the wind was revealing more of her beauty than she cared to discover. She strove to conceal her ankles, and commenced to walk off in the sheriff's direction—a movement which had the effect of rousing Usher to the necessity of making a bold stroke with his club.

" 'Fore! Miss Durie," he called out, and she stepped aside till he had delivered his blow, when he joined her. "I am playing," he said, " with Nixon's clubs. You know, I suppose, that he has given up all these vanities, and has taken himself off—heaven only knows where ? "

" But you are his friend, are you not ? You know where he has gone, and why ? "

She questioned him with so obvious an anxiety for the absent Nixon that he realized, not without discomfort to his vanity, that she had probably joined him on the links to discuss him.

" Joseph is wild," he said ; " he won't tame. He hates restraint. He was made for an open-air life—

for mountaineering and that sort of thing ; a kind of good wild animal ; and I've no doubt he will be very much happier adopting a vagabond life than pacing the Parliament House. He really never would have done anything there worth speaking about."

" I suppose it is easy to be philosophical about one's neighbours' misfortunes," said Mina.

"He hasn't shown yet whether it is to be a misfortune. How can you tell ? "

" You must know that it is a misfortune for me, Mr. Usher—the greatest—one of the greatest—trials I have been called to endure."

" Come along, come along ! " shouted the sheriff, standing impatiently at his hole, which he had taken in three shots, while his opponent had numbered eight. " Mina," he added, " I'm not at all certain that you improve the game with your presence."

"Shall I go away, then ? " she asked, decidedly offended at her reception, and grateful to Usher, who vehemently called out—

"Certainly not, my dear Miss Durie."

"Again I call that a magnificent drive," said Usher, as the sheriff started off for the next hole, his ball spinning into space before him.

Mina stood with Usher, and watched his next drive with curiosity. It was a fine strong drive, but the blast caught it, and the ball disappeared behind a high wall.

"I've lost my hole," said the advocate. "Somehow, playing with the sheriff seems to put me out. I never can do anything, and I should very much have liked to show off a little before you. Because I can play at times."

"It is very ingenuous of you to say so. But why, if I may go back upon what you say of Mr. Nixon, your friend, why do you speak of him so lightly, as a vagabond and what not?"

"Because Joe is a vagabond, using the word, of course, in its harmless sense. He is, for some reason or other, the most restless of men."

"For the same reason as I am the most restless of

women. If, Mr. Usher, you did not know, as we do not, where we have come from, you would not find life so sure and satisfactory."

"It's enough for me that we all come from the Infinite," said Usher, thinking of the snuffy little man who had thrashed him in his boyhood, and to whom he owed the debt of paternity.

"So, I suppose, does this north wind which is blowing on us, but really to me that is not the slightest consolation. What may not one have lost in being thrown upon the world without knowledge of one's parents!"

"Ah! well, from that point of view, there is something to be said for a father and mother. What one may have lost—estates, perhaps a kingdom, august relatives—who knows?"

"I didn't mean that. I meant, how much of early affection, how much of tenderest association to warm our hearts with, as life goes by."

"Well, talking of Nixon, I should say that he is no

worse off than scores and hundreds and thousands of people who have been orphaned in early youth, or even born posthumous."

"Yes, but they *know*. Nixon does not. I do not. And the result is a perpetual unsatisfied hunger to be told—just to have one little word flung us."

"From the Infinite?"

"From anywhere. One little word to say, 'You are So-and-so, and Such-and-such.'"

"Perhaps it would not be so amusing for Nixon, if he really knew. For you—if I may allude to a subject that I know must be painful to you—for you it would be important. But, in the meantime, is not Sheriff Durie father enough, and does he not satisfy all the unsatisfied yearnings by his kindness of heart? Ties——"

"Come along! come along!" shouted the sheriff, starting for a new hole at the end of the links, as he observed that Usher had practically abandoned the game, and, with his club on his shoulder, seemed to be lecturing his ward in an instructive bar manner.

"Papa is calling," said Mina, and Usher, taking a fresh ball from his pocket, renewed the game.

"You will excuse me for saying it, Usher, but I feel as if I was playing whist with a dummy. You are not exerting yourself; you are letting the game go. Mina, I'm bound to say that I think your appearance on the field has put him out. You are making him talk when he should be otherwise engaged. He threw that ball away simply because he was listening to you instead of calculating the force of the wind."

"Well, papa dear, I shall go back to my friends," said Mina; "but there is Omond with the carriage already," she added, "in front of the river."

"Omond must just cool his heels on his box, then, till we have played one round of the links. I am in brilliant condition. I've come down all this distance in six strokes. Now, Usher, let me see some play, and give me the feeling of the fight."

The wind blew more strongly; Mina retired to the carriage, and sat in it outside the Bruntsfield Arms; the two men went the round, and in three-quarters of an hour joined her.

"Beat him to sticks," said the sheriff, taking his seat, while Usher paid the caddies and carried in the clubs to the house. "Briefs are decidedly more in Frank's line than play," remarked the sheriff in his absence, "though I have seen him do better than he has done to-day. Tell him to go round home by Donaldson's Hospital, will you, Usher, if you please. You can stay all night, of course?"

"I've made no arrangements for it. Never brought a bag or anything."

"Oh, you can have one of my night-shirts, and I daresay my feet are no neater than yours—a pair of my slippers will fit you. I expect it will be a boisterous night to return in. I will let you have the carriage in the morning."

Usher looked at Mina as if he expected the in-

vitation to be emphasised. She said nothing, however, and her silence decided him. Yes, he would go
out to Durie Den, and stay till next day. He would
not want the carriage in the morning. He needed
just such a walk to brace him up for his work, of
which he had a sufficient quantity in hand. Mina
heard his intention without the least alteration of
demeanour; she sighed, however, as the horses
trotted off, to think that the sheriff had never
asked Joseph to stay all night when he came out to
see them. It was a pleasant room to dine in—the
sheriff's: the lights were so well subdued, the log on
the hearth was so resinous, and crackled and blazed
so cheerily; the dinners were so unostentatious, yet
so sound and good in every detail, and the sheriff's
father looked out of his oil portrait on the table
with so jovial a recognition of guests. Usher felt
that to be in that dining-room, helped by the light
of Mina's eyes, and encouraged by the sheriff's cheery
voice, was indeed to be in a good place. He found

himself talking brilliantly among the silver candle-sticks, about all sorts of subjects, from the discovery of gold among the northern mountains, to the quality of the last joke uttered from the Inner House. The sheriff did not believe in Scotch gold, nor did Mina, nor did Usher, in his heart of hearts; but he believed in it for argument's sake, and he argued elaborately, having fortified himself a night or two earlier with all the information about gold contained in a tattered *Encyclopædia Britannica* which he had picked up cheap in a shop on the Mound.

"It's a singular thing," said the sheriff, "that Sir Thomas Dunbeath's estate should be the seat of this new excitement. The stupid fellow went away, as you know, for some unexplained reason, about eighteen years ago."

" Was the reason unexplained ?"

"Quite, Mina; pass the claret to Frank. I must tell you the history of that claret by-and-by. It's part of a brand purchased by a west country iron-

master, when he was touring in France. He went
into a vineyard one day, and, having tasted, asked,
'What dy'e sell that at?' He was told, and laconi-
cally observed, 'Send me the year's growth to the
Clyde!' That's part of the year's growth; very good, .
isn't it? These moneyed fellows are always doing
sublime things of that sort. I suppose it's power.
Oh! yes, to be sure, we were talking of Sir Thomas
Dunbeath. Do I recollect him? Perfectly. A gentlemanly man, much liked by everbody, who pinned
his faith too much to Leslie, in those days rather a
younger man than he is now. There were rumours—
all kind of gossiping talk about Sir Thomas having
contracted this, that, and the other secret marriage.
In truth the mysterious disappearance of Sir Thomas
is still credited to his having been overmuch married,
in those days of his hot youth. I give no credence to
the gossip, Mina; you needn't look so shocked."

"I hear some rumours," said Usher, "of Leslie
displeasing the Estates Court with his arbitrary ways,

and of some new man being appointed to take up his work at Ruddersdale."

" Impossible !—keep the ironmaster's claret circulating—impossible, my dear fellow. Leslie is essential to the district. No court would dare to supersede him, at least in the present shifty state of affairs. The Crown may do what it likes when it gets them, but Leslie's as much a fixture as Cnoc Dhu."

" What are his views about Sir Thomas ? "

" That he will return."

" Does he believe in what gossip says of him and his marriage ? "

" He thinks there is an heir, if we could only trace Sir Thomas." The sheriff was eating a bunch of grapes at that moment. Mina rose and left the room. Usher leaned across the table with a look of uncontrollable excitement. " Who," he asked, " is Mina Durie, if she be not Mina Dunbeath ? "

CHAPTER X.

"AULD ACQUAINTANCE."

MR. LESLIE, of Ruddersdale, met Oliver Gun at the wooden bridge in the "strath," and went up the burn with him to the shieling. Elspeth pointed out to him where she had collected the sand from which the particles were taken. Unfortunately, however, that red sky in the morning, which is the shepherd's warning, had betokened a storm. Cnoc Dhu sent down his swollen waters with a rush, and the ridge which had been left on the banks melted away like snow. It was in vain that Mr. Leslie took up handful after handful of hard pebbles and scrutinised them. They were the common round pebbles of the Marnock streams, and no suggestion of ore in them.

"You," he said, after a few hours of painful search, "you remarked, with some of that native shrewdness which belongs to you, that you never tell a lie except when you can't help it. Now, oblige me by saying if you think there has been any necessity for telling a lie on the present occasion. We understand each other, I think. Has there been any lie about this gold? Did those grains you brought me come out of this stream?"

"I can assure you, sir, that every grain of them came out of the burn. Elspeth has the bottom of the snuffbox filled with them again; but she has to be very cautious with her mother——"

"Ay?"

"Her mother has a great aversion to the gold; she says that it's not canny, and no good can ever come of it."

"Maybe her mother's not so far wrong. What do you want gold for, on the side of Cnoc Dhu? You can get as much 'braxy' as you like without it. It's us of the town who need the gold, not you. But just tell Elspeth to bring me that snuffbox, will you?"

The box was brought him, and there was no doubt about the contents. The particles were perfectly pure.

"Your wife doesn't like it, Gun; here's a crisp, new pound note to you. Give me these grains."

The shepherd was overpowered with gratitude.

"I'll be coming into the town to live," he said, "if I'm going to pick up money so fast."

Mr. Leslie gave him a sharp, suspicious look; "You fool!" he said, "are you not very well off where you are? Your wife has more sense in her little finger than there is in your whole body. A little gold soon turns your head. What would you do coming into town?"

"Elspeth's getting to be a young woman, now," he replied, "and she likes to be in the town, whiles."

"Let me hear no more of this," said Mr. Leslie, with a harshness in the intonation of his voice which made the shepherd start where he stood.

Nothing more was said on the subject, and the

factor, having taken tea in the shieling, went back to the bridge, where his horse was fettered, and returned to Ruddersdale.

Some nights afterwards he sat in his dining-room, which overlooked the square, his table covered with papers. Mr. Leslie's dining-room was spacious, a window at either end of it, well curtained; the furniture upon the most massive scale, as if it were made for perpetuity, and the lights dim. He had never consented to gas being introduced into the town, and Mr. Leslie's room was more dim than religious in its lighting. In his dining-room above the bank, he was waiting for a visitor. While he waited, he turned occasionally the leaf of a letter, and lifted his head from its perusal with a jerk, as if he were stung. The letter annoyed him; and though he had eaten and drunk, as he usually did, till his stomach was loaded and his brain spun with wine, he could not command the drowsiness which so often relieved him. The letter ran:

“MY DEAR LESLIE,—A suggestion has been made to me by one of the most promising advocates, during a private conversation, that compels me to ask you one or two questions. We were discussing Cnoc Dhu and the rumours of gold and the prospect of a new industry being established at your door. Sir Thomas Dunbeath’s name naturally came up, and I described his character to my friend, the advocate. Putting matters together, he suddenly startled me by the question—‘Who is Mina Durie, if she be not Mina Dunbeath?’ It is many years now since I have given up thinking who Mina is. It is enough for me that she is the light of my life, that she has grown up at my fireside since first I took charge of her, shedding upon my home every gracious influence. But I owe her so much that I live in dread of doing her an injustice. If by any chance the cloud which obscures her birth should roll aside, I shall not seek to darken the discovery through a selfish affection for the girl. I should rather be pleased to find for her the parentage she so much misses, though I have done my best to make her forget antecedents. Give me then, the following information. First, is the man still alive who brought her to you from the foreign wreck? Where was Sir Thomas Dunbeath, to the best of your knowledge, during the storm? Is the old woman still alive who unwound the strips of the deed of conveyance from the child's body? I know you have no faith in tracing Mina's parentage; but I am forced to make these inquiries, as I have a great belief in the judgment and instinct of the advocate who suggested the possibility of her being the daughter of Sir Thomas."

Leslie read the sheriff's letter with a snort, and looked from his watch to the door. His visitor was not punctual. His irritation seemed to grow by delay. Twice he swore, as he rose, drew back the curtains, and heard the riotous laughter which was coming from the other side of the square. Then he rested himself with his letter and summoned what patience he could to his aid. He needed it; for it was an hour before Nancy Harper, dressed in full mourning, opened his dining-room door and took a seat on a distant chair.

“Why the deuce don't you keep your engagements?” he asked, tossing the sheriff's letter into the centre of his heaped table.

Mrs. Harper unfolded a clean handkerchief and wiped her brow, which was not moist, but which, she seemed to feel, was in need of mopping. Her withered hand shook; but there was an expression of hard firmness about her mouth which restrained Mr. Leslie in the more copious use of expletives.

“I misdoubted the cause of the errand, Roderick Leslie. I wad be let alone now that I am growing auld. I had hoped that there was, maybe, some peace in store for me, and that the dead past would bury its dead.”

“So, Mrs. Harper,” said the factor, rising, “you're ashamed of the help you gave me in an earlier day?

Come, cheer up. Take my keys and open that sideboard, and suit yourself. You can't go just in five minutes."

" No, no. I can hear ye without drinking with ye. What is it ye would have me listen to that ye couldn't tell me at my own ingle-nook. Have I not washed my hands, these dozen years, of all that ever concerned me with you ? "

" Come, come, Nancy," said the factor, softening a little, " for auld lang syne, ye ken. For auld lang syne, my trusty housekeeper. There has been no dead buried in the past, as you very well know. They're alive, hang them ! and up, and active, and suspicious, and wanting to know. Death !" he broke out, his brow inflaming with red wrath, as he paced the floor of his room. "Death! It was one of the chances I thought Time would give me. I thought there would be death and the grave, Nancy Harper ; and Time has not been kind."

The innkeeper shuddered as she looked at him.

"God soften ye!" she said. "And tell me quickly what it is ye would say to me. And dinna be lookin' like that, Roderick Leslie, and handling your gun when you're thinking o' human life."

"You hag!" he exclaimed; "who was thinking thoughts of that sort?"

"I've never in all my recollection of ye seen ye look so fearsome. Ah! when ye were a brawer and a younger man ye did what ye liked, and it didna misbecome ye. But ye've aged, like me, Roderick Leslie, and sin sits ill on an aging man."

"Drink, ye old fool! and keep your fine saws for finer occasions. I tell ye I'm in danger—in deep, immediate peril—and don't know when it may break upon my head, and overwhelm me. What I have done I am not ashamed of. If ever Sir Thomas Dunbeath comes back over the seas where he went, what have I to fear?"

"Twa black craws," murmured the woman.

"Nothing to fear from Sir Thomas. I did what I

did in his interest, and he would recognize it and clear me if he returned. But the law would take a different view of it. Ay, it would that, Nance; and you and I—we would have to leave our bonny bields at Ruddersdale, and serve our time at the crank and the treadmill with people that we have never been used to consort with—not very respectable people—no, no;" and Roderick Leslie, half chuckling, half frowning, poured himself out more spirits, and pushed a glass of old brandy to Mrs. Harper's end of the table.

The woman's firm mouth became firmer as she turned a washy pair of grey eyes upon the speaker.

"I washed my hands o' all your secrets a dozen years ago," she said, sustaining herself with the brandy; "and indeed I wish to go down the hill quietly, and no to be fashed with them again."

Leslie stopped in his pacing, and filled the room with laughter which was as loud and discordant as it was empty of true mirth.

"No to be fashed, Nancy!   Ha, ha, ha!—no to be fashed.   But if Sir Thomas Dunbeath doesn't come back to say that in sending his heir to Jericho I was acting up to his instructions, then, if certain things happen that look as if they might happen, fashed you will need to be.   The law allows of no repentance, Nancy Harper, for a deed done which has never been expiated.   It takes account of nothing but the deed done."

"God send the baronet home again!"

"The devil take him, that he ever left me to take up the task of suppressing his lies!   But you had a hand in it.   The law would hold you responsible for half of the act.   It would, indeed.   And ye canna be fashed!   Ha, ha, ha!"

"It's an ill-timed merriment, Roderick Leslie.   It's no' the laugh of a repentant man who was trying (as many's the time you have told me you were) to get a' things right, so that at your death Ruddersdale might come back to its own owner."

"Read that," said Leslie abruptly, tossing her Sheriff Durie's letter. He watched her as she read. He saw the tears steal into her eyes, and her cheeks become moist. He noted that the hard, firm mouth relaxed, and he listened to her murmuring—

"Poor simple gentleman. Oh, the poor lamb! Verily, the way of the transgressor is hard—hard!"

"Now, attend to me," he said, when he got tired of watching the play of Nancy's features. "You observe that this soft-hearted old fool doesn't want a parentage for his girl. With his 'light of his life' and his 'gracious influence,' and his cant of affection, Nance, he'd better fall in love with her, and come up with her to the court next time as Mrs. Durie."

The woman raised her hands to her eyes, rubbed them as if in a dream, rose in her chair, and shooting at him a glance of scorn, exclaimed,—

"Haud! Roderick Leslie, you may go too far. I'm but a puir auld woman, and naebody dependin' to me but my dead husband's feyther. It may be the crank or the treadmill to me for what I helped you to do eighteen long years ago; but I helped you in the belief that out of evil good would come; and if you breathe to me such a word as you have said, I will put myself in the hands o' them that will look into the whole circumstances, and be it death or prison await me, I will take them."

"You are forgetting what a jovial fellow I am, Nance Harper, what a wild wit and humour I have, and how it bubbles over and explodes in spite of me. No! Sheriff Durie shall not marry her. But now, about another subject connected with this. The diggers who came by the mail-coach are still with you, I suppose?"

"Aye, puir fellows."

"Do they get letters? Does the younger of the two, the man Nixon, correspond with the south?"

"No, no! they have no letters, if it isn't a letter Mr. Russell gets from his wife. They're intent upon the goold, Mr. Leslie. I think from rising in the morning to going to their bed at night, there's nothing in their heads but goold — goold — goold. Sirs the day, Ruddersdale's daft. To think of how it fills auld heads and young alike; and I'm thinking its many a barrel o' silver fish that will be lost, the year, for that daftness."

"And he doesn't correspond with the south ? "

"Mr. Nixon ? "

"Yes, Mr. Nixon."

"Weel, if he disna write his letters in the open air, and put them in the box, its unbeknown to me that he writes letters."

"What sort of habits has he ? "

"Habits ? "

"Is he a big feeder ? Does he drink hard ? Does he work ? Does he make himself agreeable at your ingle-nook ? Is he a fool or a knave, or both ? Or does he pretend to be a gentleman ?"

"He's just a quiet, well-behaved, stoot Scotch lad wi' a gude appetite and halesome manners. He asks a heap o’ questions, though. And I believe he was in the law ere he cam’ here. I hear Mr. Russell give him a bit chaff now and again because he wore the wig.”

Roderick Leslie’s peregrinations through his room became more and more violent as his questions were answered. He twice helped himself to renewed quantities of spirits, and with his hand upon Nancy’s shoulder, he stopped to ask,—

“Yes! He puts questions, does he? What may they be?”

“You fear me wi’ that look o’ yours. Truly you fear me. Oh! yes, the way of the transgressor is hard.”

“Tell me, will you!” he asked, with a burst of anger, pressing his heavy right hand on her lean, left shoulder, “what this well-behaved Scotch lad, with the good appetite, busies his mind with? What does he inquire about?”

“Hands off!” cried Mrs. Harper, rising and shaking herself free of his grasp, “you forget yourself. It’s a strait waistcoat you're working up to. Don't think to intimidate me. The lad just asked whether a foreign wreck had happened in the bay eighteen years ago, and if I remembered it, and if I thought there was still any of the wood of the ship left in the village, and if I remembered the babe that was taken into your house, and what kind of a man Mr. Leslie was, and what the people of the neighbourhood thought about him?"

"You answered him, I suppose, down to the minutest detail of his inquiry? You told him that you remembered the storm, that you handled the foreign babe, that—— Nancy Harper, if you betray me I will kill you."

The woman, with all her coolness and knowledge of the roughness of men, trembled where she sat. The man was transfigured with wrath, and the resolution that wrath had inspired him with to save himself at others' expense, even if his means of salvation were murder.

“ Oh ! Roderick Leslie, think twice about the road you are going. You know enough about the law and about life to take yourself oot o’ this difficulty. A bit callant wi a canoe ! and you talking about shedding of blood.”

Leslie recovered himself, but there was no abatement in his anger, as he ordered her “ to watch this Nixon, find out all that happened to him, and bring her account of it to him.” A little later he stopped in front of his mirror, and the figure he saw was that of a wild beast thirsting for blood.

CHAPTER XI.

NIXON'S DISCOVERY.

As an experienced miner, Russell took it upon him
to direct operations. He asked Nixon to take an
accurate note of the Rudder from its source to the sea.
It was a day's journey to the source in his canoe, for
the Rudder started from the sedges of a loch round
the foot of Cnoc Dhu. He was to keep in his mind
all the shingle margins and stretches of sand, all the
cliffs of granite and clay banks where easy spade-
work might bring to view the boasted ore of the
stream. Nixon was not a geologist; but all the
geological survey required for Russell's purpose he
was quite competent to perform. Moreover, he liked
doing the work. Surveying was greatly more to his

mind than that harder task of sinking shafts which lay before him. Not that he was afraid of his work, having undertaken it, but, being a new kind, the preliminaries to it pleased him more than he thought the work would do itself. Besides, canoeing had been the dearest enjoyment of his life, and, on the Rudder, he had every variety of exercise. There were shallows to annoy him, in which he sometimes rasped the stones, and was jerked forward, paddle in hand, till his face touched the bow. There were long murky pools, where the water was black, over which he sped as if on wings. There were plunging rapids, in which the waves roared and foamed, and the spray, shot with the hues of the rainbow, rolled round the banks like the steam from a cauldron. Each variation of the stream had its own peculiar kind of excitement, and in contrast to the odour of his empty brief-box he had the air of the heather. No wonder, then, he felt an unwonted exuberance as one day he rounded the foot of Cnoc Dhu, and paddled into the quiet waters of Loch Dirlot. There was not so much as a ripple on the brown surface, and the wide plain of water suddenly revealed to him lay tranquil at the foot of Cnoc Dhu's crags, as if never wind visited it. And the crags! They went sheer up, pillared and shelved and fissured, until the sheep at the top became mere wandering specks of wool. Instead of silence, too, as he had expected, the air was full of the cry of wild birds, not a melodious cry, certainly, but angry skirling, accompanied by a noisy beating and wheeling of wings. He turned idly in his canoe. There was an island not far off; the birds were rising from it in clouds and urging their way towards the cliff; the first greenness of spring was showing amongst the herbage; he idly paddled towards it. He leapt ashore on a beach of shingle, where he saw a boat moored. He looked into the boat, and in a willow basket his eye caught sight of a great collection of eggs. They seemed to be every hue, size, and shape. Some of them were of an exquisitely pale violet; others had red lines and freckles; some were snowy white, some sea-green with inky streaks; they were all the eggs of large birds, and, as Nixon looked at them, he understood why it was that at the farther end of the island there was so violent a demonstration on the wing. Being fatigued with his long row, however, he did not go to see. He preferred to rest himself on the shingle and to call to mind that he had come there for gold.

"I don't know that this would be a bad place," he reflected, laying out a flask and burying the head of his pipe in the inside of his pouch while he deftly filled it with his thumb. "This is alluvium I suppose, and I shall report to Russell that we had better come here and dig. Heavens! what a place to dig; with that magnificent mountain looming over us. I wonder how many aspects Cnoc Dhu has? I have seen five or six already. I must go round the northern side and look at that. Well, well! and not a human being to see it except the old Highlander who is stirring up strife among the birds. I sha'n't be sorry to see a human face again."

Puff, puff, puff! Having pulled at his flask he sat, with his hands clasped, puffing into the tranquil air, feeling inside him such a tranquillity as only these remote spots can bring. He had not to wait long before a crackling among the twigs behind him announced the presence of the disturber of the peace of the island. He had expected an old Highlander, with a shrivelled face and a pair of watery, startled dark eyes. But no, this was no Highlander who walked down the strand, her apron loaded with eggs; it was a girl with the flush of excitement on her cheeks, and her grey eyes shone, and as she lifted out her willow basket from her boat and put in the eggs, Nixon rose to his feet, making a noise among the shingle. The girl turned, and such was her surprise at the sight of him that she dropped some of her spoil at her feet, and drew back with an air of defiant surprise. She was dressed in homely cotton, and her hair was gathered within a sun-bonnet the colour of a buttercup; she stood looking at him in wonder for a little while, until she saw his canoe and paddle, when she overcame her surprise and smiled.

Nixon smiled, too. "Yes, I came over in that," he said, withdrawing his pipe to speak, and walking towards her across the shingle.

"You'll be a gauger?" she said.

"I wish I was," he answered. "I'm not in such an important position."

"You'll be one of the Duke's people?"

"Guess again. I'm not one of his people."

"You'll be a stranger?"

"Yes, that's my profession."

"What airt did ye come from?"

"I came round the foot of Cnoc Dhu. How did you come?"

"The same way."

"Are you one of the Duke's people?"

" No."

" You'll not be a stranger ? "

" No."

" I shouldn't think you were very popular on the
island. The birds were rather scared by your presence. Do they always skirl when they see you ? "

" Yes, indeed they do. They know very well
when they see me and my boat that there'll be a
thinning amongst the eggs."

" You'll be a Highland young lady ? "

" No, I'm not Highland, suppose that I live at
Cnoc Dhu. My father's Lowland, and my mother's
Lowland too. He came up from the town."

" Which one ? "

" Ruddersdale town. There's not any other one
near. Do you not know Ruddersdale ? "

" I am living at it."

" And is there any news, then, from the town ? "

She sat down on the gunwale of the boat—a big,
awkward, lumbering boat, with heavy oars—and

seemed inclined to chat. Nixon strolled towards her, and was very willing to prolong the conversation. He did not think it was treason to Mina Durie to notice that beneath the buttercup sun-hat her hair rippled and shone. He did not forget Mina because he looked at her grey eyes and saw that they were clear and sincere.

"What sort of news would you like?"

"Oh! it's not what I would like; it's what's going on. It's a real queer thing to ask me what I would like, as if the news would happen because you said it."

"Ah! I think you must be a Highland young lady."

"Indeed I am not. It's the Mackays that are Highland. The Guns are all Lowland. And in this country if you are not a Gun you are a Mackay; and if you are not a Mackay you are a Gun."

"Well, let me see! News. Do you know Mrs. Harper?"

"Oh! if I don't. Nancy and me, we are the best friends in the world. I like old Nancy Harper, and I live there when I go to the town."

"This morning early, then, I looked out of my window—the window above the doorway, with the white blind and muslin curtains—"

"Oh! never:" said the girl; "if it isn't the very room I had myself when I was in the town."

"I don't dislike it because of that," said Nixon, who did not forget the sheriff's ward.

"Why would you dislike it because of that? I'm Oliver Gun's daughter, and he's the best shepherd in the north."

"But I was giving you the news."

"Pardon me then, but though we live on the mountain-side we're very proud and take offence easy. Now let me hear the news."

"Well, I looked out of window, and saw a man in his shirt sleeves go down the pier, light a pipe, smoke, and go home again. I saw another man do the same. Then more smoke began to rise from the cabin of a smack in the harbour. Then the morning mail-coach from the north passed, with Mr. Laggan at the back of it, blowing his horn till his red cheeks seemed swollen to the bursting. After that, I went out on the pier myself, smoked, had my breakfast, walked off with my canoe under my arm, and came on here."

"Oh, well! that's not very much news you've brought."

"You don't manufacture it on a large scale at Ruddersdale."

"If it was the fishing season you wouldn't say that. There's plenty of news then; and I was expecting that there would be news about the gold."

Nixon looked at her curiously.

"You have heard of the gold, then?"

"Heard of it!" tossing her head proudly. "I discovered it. It was me who found it first. And it was my father and me who took it to Mr. Leslie. My father went in, and I waited outside at the door. To be sure, I have heard of the gold. See, too, that medal, with a hole in it, that I'm wearing. He gave me that for what I found in my basin."

The girl pulled a sovereign from her throat, where it was suspended, and showed it to Nixon, who approached and bowed his head over her bosom to look at it. He looked longer at the sovereign than he required to do in order to master the details of its date of publication. The girl replaced it with a gesture of importance, exclaiming :—

" I think it's me that has more news than you, though you have come from the town."

" Why," he pursued, after a while, looking at her soft arm, "how did you get that?"

Her arm was bare, and just below the elbow the blood flowed from an abrasion of the skin.

" The birds are so tame on the island that some of them won't move ; and I had to stir up a great wild-goose with my foot to get her to get up, and when she wouldn't budge with my foot, I had to put down my arm and lift her off. She turned round and gave me a good nip."

"Yes; I should say it was. Let me wash it for you."

The girl laughed, and said: "Now I have got all my eggs I will be going."

"You are in a desperate hurry to be off."

"I've been here a good while, and I have to take them back to my father's house on Cnoc Dhu, for he has to blow them and sort them on strings before he takes them down to Duncan Elder's. Oh no, they're not for eating at all. They're for selling to strangers, like you. We couldn't eat them for the taste of the fish is so strong in them. But the strangers buy them for curiosity, and Duncan Elder —he's not on our land at all; he's a forester on the Duke's property—he gives my father half of what they will give him. So you see, I'm not coming here for nothing."

"I should like, if you don't mind, to give that wild goose a knock on the head if you would show me where she is sitting."

"What would be the use of that? Is it because she gave me a nip? Never mind her. It's a provoking thing for them to have their eggs taken away from them. I must be off now, or my father will be getting anxious. You see he hasn't so much time at this season of the year, what wi' the young lambs coming, and the sheep wanting to go up Cnoc Dhu again after the winter months."

"I'm going back your way; I'll accompany you so far," he said, as she stepped nimbly into her boat, and threw out the unwieldy oars on either side.

"The birds *are* in a rage," she said, as a storm of screaming broke over their heads. "I'll be glad to get out of this noise."

They rowed out of the loch, almost abreast of each other, she looking curiously at his frail craft and deft

paddle, he expressing a little anxiety at the dead
weight of her oars and the Dutch heaviness of her
boat. They were not long in reaching the Rudder,
which emerged among sedges from the loch, and
dawdled slowly down towards the sea.

"Ah, I just thought that my father would be
getting anxious," pointing to a figure with a crook on
the margin of the stream.

"And that's Oliver Gun, is it?"

CHAPTER XII.

THE OPINION OF HER FRIENDS.

SHERIFF DURIE was not very grateful to Frank
Usher for the suggestion he had made about Mina.
He would have preferred that Mina should remain
on his hands as much a problem as the originator
of the origin of species, the man in the iron mask
and the author of Junius. But his mind was too
much habituated to the search for cool truth to
allow him to ignore any suggestion which seemed
to be made in good faith. Usher had made the
suggestion that Mina was the daughter of Sir Thomas
Dunbeath with something like passion. The sheriff
was not unaware that the advocate saw what an
advantage Nixon had in devoting himself to her

service, and that he was anxious accordingly to assert his own interest in the search. Both the young men bored him on the subject, but Usher less than Nixon, because he regarded him as a brilliant youth, with solid prospects. He was not sorry, however, having written to his friend, Leslie, in the North to hear that the man or men who had brought Mina ashore from the wreck had long left the coast, though the woman who had nursed Mina was still available for cross-examination in her little inn at Ruddersdale. Had he been thoroughly disinterested, the sheriff would not have been pleased to find that some of the avenues to the truth were permanently closed. He thought, however, he was old enough to know that even if Mina did discover her true parentage, she would never be happier than she had been in his house. He was more than usually brisk and alert on the morning of Leslie's answer, and after breakfast, as he stood looking on the spring sunlight, in which the insects were beginning to come to life about his lawn, he hummed tunes. Dressed in a velvet shooting coat, with a blue tie on his breast, he seemed more like an artist than a distributor of judgments. Mina knew whenever he made his appearance in that style that he was unusually well and cheerful.

"I haven't done anything at my 'Eminent Scotch Sheriffs' for some months, Mina," he remarked, wheeling round upon her. He had been engaged for twenty years upon a book purporting to bear that title. Somehow it never got written, though the reputation of it had gone abroad, and people were accustomed to say of him, "What! Don't know Sheriff Durie! He's written the most masterly account of the Scotch sheriffry which exists." That is what he meant they should say, having completed the book. As yet, however, after twenty years' consideration of it, he had got no farther than ten fragments of biography, in which he thought he had turned some very good periods, and written in-

cidental passages of history worthy of Alison or
Macaulay. Though the book never got itself completed, it kept the sheriff a good deal in the
Advocates' Library, and he was not a little proud
of the voluminous quantity of extracts he had made
in the course of the twenty years' consideration he
had given to the subject. "I don't get on as I
would wish to," he said, diving both hands into the
pockets of his coat, and turning upon Mina, who
stood enveloped in a dark dress of velveteen edged
with gold—she was preparing to go out, and make
some morning calls. He was delighted to see that
the craving for a little social life had come back
upon her. She had not recently cared much about
going out. "I must take it up again, Mina. The
administration of Scotch law during the Reformation
period—that is the knotty portion I am writing,
and it requires a great deal of hard burrowing. I
must get help. Indeed Usher has been good enough
to give me a little help already. It's a singular

circumstance about Usher, what an entire absence of the historical sense there is in him. He sees a precedent and its application to a given case with mighty keenness. But the nice proportion, the feeling for antiquity, and the style which are requisite for my 'Eminent Scotch Sheriffs,' are entirely denied him."

"I am sure Joseph had nice proportion."

"Oh, come Mina, that's too much of a good thing. Joseph knew—knows, I should say—quite less about Scotch history than a town messenger. Quite less! Don't look so gloomy. I am very far from underrating Joseph on his own ground. But as for giving me any assistance in my 'Eminent Scotch Sheriffs,' oh no! Now, I am not likely to be back before dinner-time; where do you propose to go to? Don't call upon that sour old Mrs. Gibson. She'll only fill your mind with bitterness. She's a disagreeable woman. An unwholesome, unsatisfactory, entirely obnoxious woman. I hope she will remove out of the neighbourhood, and take her scandal-mongering into some community which will better appreciate it."

"No, papa dear, I sha'n't call on her. I like her as little as you do. I mean to walk round and see the Finlays. Perhaps I shall go as far as the Bertrams."

"Then you will want to ride?"

"No; I shall prefer to walk round. It is a lovely morning. Bessie Finlay will expect me, and Gerty, too."

"Very good," said the sheriff, his head full of his eminent predecessors; "only I suppose you will be back at dinner."

"At dinner, yes."

The sheriff drove into town, and Mina walked a mile round the hill to the Finlays. The Finlays have nothing to do with Mina's subsequent history, as they had nothing to do with her past. She only went there because they were neighbours, Mr. Finlay being a personage who ran steamboats from Leith to every known port between the north and south pole. Mr. Finlay was an abstraction to Mina, a fat abstraction, who came home in his carriage at seven o'clock in the evening, who dined by himself, and rolled away—nobody ever having seen much of him in the interval—next morning at eight o'clock. He had, however, four pretty daughters, the major part of whose life was spent at Corstorphine, between a green lawn, a hot-house, a drawing-room, and their bedrooms. Their father was very nearly as much an abstraction to them as to Mina. He never said good-morning to them in the morning; he never kissed them at night when they went to their beds; he sometimes called Gerty Bessie, and Bessie Gerty, having no very sustained idea in his mind who was who. Perhaps it was because his wife had borne him fifteen daughters in his time, and the survivors were not unlike some of the deceased. At any rate, Mina liked them, though she knew little of their father, and she valued their opinion on most of those questions which pretty girls discuss when they see each other, on green lawns, in hot-houses, or in their bedrooms.

"Oh, lovely!" cried Gerty Finlay at a window opening upon a garden walk, where Mina was sauntering.

"Good-morning, Gerty. Isn't it lovely ? It might be mid-summer. The air is so warm and soft. I see your rookery is all finished."

"Oh, lovely!" repeated Gerty. "And it isn't the air, nor the rookery. It's you, Mina. Bessie, do look, before she comes nearer."

The two sisters, brown-haired, clear-complexioned girls, stood at the window and looked down at Mina, who smiled upon them. As she went to the door Gerty said to Bessie—

"I'm sure she is a foreign princess. Did you ever see anything so becoming as that walking dress ? "

"Oh, lovely!" cried Gerty, as Mina went into their morning-room, where they were snipping the stalks of flowers and arranging them prettily for bestowal over the house.

"Gerty, don't," cried Mina; "please restrain your admiration. You make me feel quite unhappy. What is it? Is it the lace, or the shape, or——"

"It's everything put together, Mina dear, and yourself looking for all the world like a foreign princess."

Mina knew that her neighbours busied themselves with making up little romances about her origin. But she did not care to be reminded of it. She preferred to move out and in among them as Sheriff Durie's daughter.

"Turn round, Mina," said Bessie, "and give me a back view."

Mina turned round to oblige her, and then sat down, positively declining to be admired or criticised any longer.

Mrs. Finlay came in presently—a large solid woman with a jovial expression of worldly enjoyment, and was invited to take up the strain commenced by Gerty at the open window.

"And, how's the sheriff?" asked Mrs. Finlay.

"Over head and ears in work," said Mina.

"Ah, it's a very exacting profession, the law," said Mrs. Finlay, scrutinising the girl from top to toe; adding, "I do think Bessie, that a walking-dress like that would suit your complexion and figure better than it does Mina's. Now, if I were dressing you, Mina, I should say, 'Choose colours which by contrast bring out your own natural complexion.' That's a good rule, and though you are raven dark, you dress yourself in dark material, which is a mistake. No doubt the yellow edging relieves it, and the lace is pretty in any case at your throat and your wrists. Still, something lighter would suit my idea of you better. It would make the most of your raven hair and your delicate complexion. But, after all, you're an engaged girl, and it doesn't much matter."

"Mama, you're always telling people unpalatable truths," said Bessie.

"Is it an unpalatable truth to be told that you are engaged? I can assure you, Bessie, I shouldn't be at all sorry to be telling you just such a truth."

Bessie snipped her flowers contemptuously, and remarked that "she was not such a hopeless old maid that her mama should be so desperately anxious to have her engaged."

"They don't go off," pursued Mrs. Finlay without the least apparent idea that she was saying anything annoying, "they don't go off, Mina. I don't know whether it's their noses or their feet, but nobody proposes for them. I did think that the engaging young publisher who danced six waltzes with her at the December assembly had some intention of proposing. But no. It all ended in his calling upon Mr. Finlay and asking him for cheap rates for his books to the Cape of Good Hope."

"There's nothing the matter with our noses," said

Gerty, feeling that organ with her thumb and finger, and talking in a nasal voice.

"Don't you think," pursued Mrs. Finlay, "that Gerty has got rather too much nose for the shape of her face? It makes her look so decided and sometimes quite repulsively firm ; whereas, poor thing, she is a perfect angel of acquiescence, and would be a treasure to any reasonable man. Bessie's nose is not the thing either. I like a nose like yours, now, Mina ; that, if you will excuse me for saying it, suggests a little reserve of impudence."

"Oh, ma!" cried Gerty, "Mina is not——"

But the mother was not going to be stopped in the high career of her talk.

"Well, you are an engaged girl at any rate, Mina, and you can tell them if it isn't a very happy time of life. I wasn't long engaged myself. Mr. Finlay married me six weeks after he saw me. That was before he had steamboats. He was always a hasty man, but though we married in haste we never repented at leisure. Long engagements are a mistake. I have no patience with a man who asks a girl to be his wife, and keeps her dilly-dallying for years till he is ready; life isn't long enough for that sort of thing. When is your marriage coming off? Dear me, I forget whether it is that strong young man, Nixon, or that disgustingly clever advocate, Usher, you are engaged to."

"Ma rattles away," said Bessie: "you mustn't mind her, Mina. She's been so much about the world with pa that she says anything just for the sake of talk."

"I am not thinking much about marriage," said Mina, gulping down a strange sensation at her throat.

"You take it very seriously to be an engaged girl, Mina," said Mrs. Finlay. "I remember when I was engaged I made faces at myself in the looking-glass one half of the day, and kissed Alec the other half."

"Ma, dear, I think you are rather coarse," said Bessie, looking at Mina's disturbed countenance.

" Well, I'm not porcelain, I admit that. What does the sheriff think of your marriage, my dear ? Here are the Bertrams, I declare—Bobby Bertram and his sister. He's an idle lad, that Bobby Bertram. Gerty, go upstairs for my thimble. Well, Bobby Bertram, how are you ? How do you do, Eleanor ? We were just discussing Mina's engagement."

" Dear Mrs. Finlay, please not to discuss it any longer," said Mina.

" I was saying, Eleanor, that I think it's their noses which keeps them from going off—I mean my girls. I have no fault to find with Mina's nose."

Bobby Bertram, an extravagantly-dressed youth, carrying a heavy flavour of scent about him, twirled his dark moustache and looked sentimentally at Mina.

" Bobby, when are you going to do any work ? ' asked Mrs. Finlay.

" When the lawns are in order I'm going to devote my time to croquet."

"How would you like to be engaged to an advocate?" asked Mrs. Finlay, addressing Eleanor.

Mina looked miserable, but it was no use attempting to restrain Mrs. Finlay. She was nothing if not outspoken. Eleanor was a tall girl, with a good figure and a malevolent face. She said if one didn't marry a publisher, one must marry an advocate—there was no other choice in the metropolis; but at least she wouldn't like you to marry a man who couldn't speak up to his brief when he got one.

"I would marry for love, not for these sorts of reasons," said Gerty with a simper.

"Oh! I daresay you will run away with the baker some day," interruped her mother; proceeding to remark, "I must say, Eleanor, I think you have the right of it. Who was it, girls, told us about that Mr. Nixon, what a shameful breakdown he had made in the Parliament House?"

"Ma, I wish you would hold your tongue," exclaimed Bessie, looking at Mina's disconsolate face.

"Oh! you're all so sensitive nowadays," said Mrs. Finlay, ringing for something to eat and drink. "Here, my dear, if I haven't said the right thing about your sweetheart, I'm sorry for it. Come and sit next me. Bobby Bertram, sit at the head of the table and carve. You will be hungry after your walk. Idle people are always hungry, Bobby."

"Or thirsty, Mrs. Finlay," said Bobby, looking in the direction of the decanter.

Mina had come for a little sympathy, or, at least for a little variation to the monotony of her regret, for the absent Joseph. But here she found nothing but contempt for her absent lover. On the other hand, Usher was discussed in a strain so flattering that she felt she had done him much injustice in all her thoughts of him.

"He is very ambitious," said Eleanor Bertram; "but I love ambition in a man. One may be sure it will always take him a little way up the mountain, even if he don't reach the top. He is just the sort of man I should like to marry."

."I hate your hard-working fellows," ejaculated Bobby, who had an income of his own, and didn't need to work.

" Eat, then, Bobby," said Mrs. Finlay.

CHAPTER XIII.

THE little community of Ruddersdale was accustomed to an annual influx of strangers. They came in from remote western islands to fill the local boats at the great season of the herring-fishing. They crowded the lowland village, and having habits of their own, they once a year gave it a foreign appearance to itself. When they had passed a couple of months sailing into the North Sea, lying through the summer midnights at their nets, they went away with their wages to their crofts on another shore. From time immemorial Ruddersdale had been used to them; it expected them; and when they came it understood their ways.

But what was this the shepherd's daughter at Cnoc Dhu had done? She had found a handful of particles, and all of a sudden Ruddersdale had blazed into the firmament of publicity. People in the south talked about Ruddersdale, wrote about Ruddersdale, waited in the great metropolis of Edinburgh for the latest news about Ruddersdale; and that, not because Ruddersdale went to sea and fished, but because gold lay among her ravines and mountains.

There was a visible increase in the importance of the leading inhabitants, as rumour magnified insignificant finds into substantial nuggets, and the hamlet gathered to itself a larger fame. In the parish church, the Rev. Mr. Johnson had Ophir constantly on his lips, and his warnings were impressive to those who set their minds upon "gear" unaccompanied by "grace." But it was enough for Ruddersdale that Mr. Leslie believed in the gold. Not that it pinned its faith in all things, temporal and spiritual, to the potentate of the place; but it had long been accustomed to his lead in everything which concerned it, and it knew of old that Roderick Leslie generally could be trusted to understand what he was about. It witnessed the arrival of a new order of face with some fear and jealousy. New arrivals who came to dig were very unlike the autumn arrivals who came to fish. The fishermen spoke Gaelic and kept much to themselves, and were, except at great pay occasions, unaffected and sober and simple. Not understanding much Scotch, they preferred their own company to the Ruddersdalers'. But the men who arrived to dig were a different order of being. Scotch they were, no doubt, like the Ruddersdalers themselves, but Scotch with all the local edge rubbed off their speech. They might have been born and bred far beyond the Border, or over the sea in Ireland, to judge from the bold incisiveness of their speech. Then they had a manner of their own. Everything they did was disagreeably " on the open." Then it was the custom of every householder in Ruddersdale to take a mid-day dram, either at Nancy Harper's, or at the big hotel, or in one or other of the spirit shops on the shore. To facilitate that object back-doors abounded in Ruddersdale, so that the " dramatists " might avoid all appearance of the evil thing when they were engaged in taking it.

It was the diplomatic homage which the " dramatists" paid to sobriety. They did not like to offend the great moral law of temperance by even seeming to take a dram. They preferred to disappear suddenly at a back-door, instead of boldly entering beneath Nancy Harper's sign, and when they reappeared in the street they liked to look as if their brief absence might be explained by the delivery of a tract, or some other similar mission of a goodly and estimable character. The new arrivals, on the contrary, were constantly dramming, but they ignored the institution of back-doors, and boldly stood, pipes in mouth and tumblers in hand, drinking, regardless of appearance or custom. Then they had no "canniness" about them, no "pawkiness"—phrases significant of the deeper diplomacies of village life ; they stood in the street, speaking right out from the chest, and that rather noisily than otherwise. They had all been at the other side of the world ; some of them had been in America ; some of them had been everywhere ; most of them professed to have already twice or thrice made large fortunes and thrown them away. It cannot be said that Ruddersdale liked them so well as it liked the quiet western fishermen ; but as the gold fever grew, it learnt to accommodate itself to them and their manners. Besides, did they not pay for their lodgings ? and was Ruddersdale to be above such a question of legitimate profit as that ? At the end of the pier a new tone was introduced into society by the diggers. Take a look at them, one of these fine spring evenings, as they stand at the pier-head, a couple of dozen of them. Russell there, and Nixon too; the latter smoking his pipe, having performed a day's rowing to Cnoc Dhu, and willing to hear the chat of the experienced before he takes up his work. There is a generic sameness about the diggers. Nixon can tell from looking at them that they have been used to spurts of hard work, varied by prolonged spells of idleness. There is one man as tall as himself sitting on a box; he has no jacket on, and he is sitting in his white shirt sleeves, and is dressed in good black cloth. What could have taken him to Ruddersdale? Not want, for ever and anon he takes out a handful of silver from his pocket to find a fusee among the change. He calls himself Armstrong, not inappropriately, to judge from the swing of his arms as he talks. Like the rest of them, he talks Scotch without any appreciable accent.

"How did I come to be at Red Gully in '52?" he is saying to a medium-sized man, wearing a beard to his waist and a belt which might have tied up a stallion. "I went mate of a brig from the Clyde the year before, and we had been dodging about the Pacific for fifteen months when we ran down to Victoria for some wool. We had heard a mighty fuss about pearls in the islands, but devil a pearl did we get; either the natives wouldn't sell or they had nothing *to* sell. Except at one remote spot, by the way, where we had—me and one o' the crew—got over a white reef, and lay off a shore where there was a mighty routing and hallooing of men and women wearing their own skins, and looking warm in them We didn't dare to land, for there were so many ot them, and they didn't seem particularly polite, the men of them handling their clubs with rather more affection than we cared about. But I noticed one old chief, wearing a pair of drawers, with a respectable kind o' look about him, though he was as blue as that sea with tattooing. So I stood up in the stern o' the boat and cried out—

"'Buono, Johnny ; hae ye ony pearls to sell ?'

"The old chap seemed to prick up his ears at that. He stepped down the beach a bit, with the dignity o' fifteen skippers. We could see by the way the crowd made way for him that he was cock o' the walk. He steps down till he stands just outside the waves, and up goes his fist, this way, and he bellows over to us— 'Hoo's a' wi' ye, my hearty?' Think o' that now, in ane o' them little Pacific islands, a tattooed man bellowing—'Hoo's a wi' ye, my hearty?' You can suppose that our first notion was to 'bout ship and run. It sounded so old Nickish. Then putting up his fist again, he calls out—'I'm frae Auchtermuchty mysel'; whaur do you come frae?'

" 'Pettycur,' says I. 'What's your name?

" 'Jock Bonthron,' says he.

" 'Jock Bonthron, o' Auchtermuchty,' says I, 'that was drooned seeven years ago?'

" 'The very same.'

" 'What are ye noo, Jock?'

" 'Come ashore and see,' he roared; and when I

was steering the boat ashore, an ugly fellow put up a boomerang above his shoulder and was going to fling, when Jock, like a hundred-weight of coal, comes down on him with his fist, and the man disappears. They were used to it, I could see, for the fellow crawled round to Jock's feet and begged his pardon. When we got ashore he takes us round to his house, as canty a bield as you'll find in Ruddersdale, and after a dish o' the finest oysters I ever tasted, and real turtle soup, he presented me wi' a handful o' pearls."

"'Armstrong,' was his last word, as he shoved us off, 'not a syllable about this to Meg.'

"'Surely, surely,' says I; for Jock had six wives and fifteen young children among the savages, and, as he said to me, 'Man, it's wonderful how comfortable you can mak' yoursel', if you just gi'e them a wee bit knockin' doon noo and again.'"

"Who was Meg?" asked Nixon.

"His weedow," replied Armstrong.

"But that's no answer to my question," suggested

the man with the leather belt; "how you came to be at the Red Gully in '52."

"I'm comin' on to that," replied Armstrong. "After we left Bonthron's island, we went due S.W. for Victoria, sure o' a cargo o' wool, at any rate; but when we threw out an anchor at Long Bay, where five-and-twenty ships lay deep in the water, we couldn't make it out at all. There wasn't a watchman aboard a single ship. Not a sign of life from stem to stern o' one o' them. Captain went ashore in his boat to look up an agent. Not a shop open. Every house deserted, every inhabitant fled, as if the plagues o' Egypt had been driving up their street. At last he came on an old Chinaman with a broken leg, and the explanation was out. "Ally go diggee goldee," said the Chinaman. Well, he went about with his boat's crew, helping himself to whatever he had a mind to; then he came aboard drunk, singing, 'Ally go diggee goldee.'

"I'll go pay a visit to that clipper lying astern,"

says I, when the captain went asleep with his head in a coal-scuttle. And off I goes, in the evening, got aboard, and what do I find? 'Witness my hand, John Boothby, that this day, my crew having deserted for the gold-fields, I follow to the same place to recover them.' Every man-jack of them had bolted, and John Boothby made the best of a bad job, and followed too. So did our crew; and that's how I came to be at Red Gully in '52."

That was only one man's chatter. There were a couple of dozen of them at it on this spring evening at the pier-head, all chattering—some of them of bloodshed and robbery; some of them of treasure made and thrown away, never to return. They were thus engaged when a stout, hectoring man, with a red face, swept down the quay.

"Take a good look at him, Nixon," said Russell.

"Why ? "

"It's Roderick Leslie; and you haven't had the pleasure of being introduced to him yet."

CHAPTER XIV.

A LITTLE TALK.

THE miners stopped their talk when Leslie made his appearance. He had evidently come down to say something to them in a body, and as a body they lifted their heads and looked at him. So cosmopolitan a group had never gathered on that pierhead before.

The local potentate seemed to be aware that he would have to throw away a little of his grand manner if he meant to be effective. It was not easy for Roderick Leslie to look anything else than an overbearing, all-powerful personage. He had it all his own way at Ruddersdale; he had no other experience than that of absolute, uncontrolled rule; he carried the marks of his experience in every movement of his person, from his stride to his frown.

"Having a little bit of a preliminary talk anent the digging—eh?" he asked, with a gracious inclination towards Russell, and a scrutinising keenness of glance in the direction of Nixon.

"We are," said all of the voices in unison.

"Now, then, you are here altogether, I want to make a proposal to you; I want you to take wages from me, and give me the use of your spades and your experience, instead of throwing it away on chance-work. I'm prepared to put down one or two thundering big shafts. Will you work for me? —say, will you take the offer? I make it to every man of you. My foreman is sitting there among you. Speak up, Russell; tell them that for me they may dig and have their victuals; for themselves they may dig and starve."

"I've been a fortnight here, Mr. Leslie," said Armstrong, "standing round your bank-door asking for a permit. I don't want wages; I want permission to dig on my own account; I can get wages anywhere. I want gold, and I'll risk the starvation."

Leslie did not answer him; he only looked steadily through the group, and said that "no permits would be issued—that all trespassers would be prosecuted."

"It's too late to say that," replied Nixon, removing his pipe, and looking at the banker. "I know two permits that are signed and paid for, and I mean to commence when I like on any shingle beach between Ruddersdale and Cnoc Dhu."

Leslie did not reply; he only looked at the speaker with narrowing eyes, then turning on his heel, as if he had been too long off his pedestal, he moved up the pier, having exclaimed—

"Settle it with Russell. He knows the terms; he will tell you how to arrange."

Then commenced a great "talkee-talkee" among the diggers, away from whom Nixon moved. He felt that he had not said enough to the banker. He must have the ground thoroughly cleared for his work, and not be hampered with thoughts of trespassing. So he followed him to the town bridge, where he was contemplating the rush of the water. As Nixon approached him he seemed to start and cower before he recovered himself to look as overbearing as usual.

"I must have this settled," said Nixon in a plain, downright way. "One of these days I shall be at work on the alluvium, and I must know that I am not to be interrupted by any of your men declaring me a trespasser."

The banker's face changed at once. He looked as near benignance as he was capable of approaching.

"Oh! Mr. Nixon, it's you. There's a difference in your case. You have my permission, sir, to dig wherever you like. I don't want to cancel the permit."

He talked as if his valleys contained gold for the picking up.

"Thanks. I'm much obliged to you."

"Oh, you are going this way too, are you?" as Nixon turned into a side path leading up the river.

"I don't mind much where I go at this hour. I had half thought of going through the plantation behind the town; but this is just as good a way as the other. I can walk with you so far."

"Thanks," said the banker with a sinister tone to his voice; "I'm much obliged to you." Nixon did not notice it. "You are putting up at Mrs. Harper's?"

"Yes; she's a good old-fashioned creature, who looks to the comfort of her guests."

"Ay."

"It's an amusing little house; I rather like living in it. There's so much goes on in it, and one hears the gossip of a hundred years in it."

"That won't do you much good."

"That depends upon circumstances—— I say, by Jove, that slip of yours very nearly sent me head-foremost into that pool."

The banker was profuse in his apologies. He had, indeed, fallen all his weight on Nixon from a side-path, and the latter only escaped from being precipitated over a crag by laying hold of an armful of gorse.

"I'm not sure that it wouldn't have finished me if I had gone in there. I can canoe that rapid, but if I had taken it headforemost—well, there's no use speculating about what might have happened: only I feel as if I had made a narrow escape from being killed. You are a good weight."

"It was a stupid and dangerous slip for me to make," said Leslie, whose jaws became unaccountably yellow as he looked at Nixon.

"Oh, don't bother about it," said the latter; "it was nothing. I was saying I liked that little house of Nancy's, because there is the gossip of a hundred years in it. I'm rather interested in Ruddersdale gossip—particularly in one incident, about which, however, it's difficult to get any light—any bright light. You remember, of course, the romance of a little girl being brought ashore from a foreign wreck, right out of a storm—a young babe who was taken over by Sheriff Durie from your hands?—I say, though, how do you happen to be looking at me in that way? You surely don't know, yourself, the expression your face wears—all thunder and jaundice. I'm not aware that I've said or done anything to incur your detestation; or are you ill?"

Leslie made some ghastly contortions of his face, said he was not very well, and had not, indeed, been able to listen to what Nixon had been saying to him. He was better now, though, and would listen. What had he to say about the romantic incident? Was he there to inquire about it? Did he know the sheriff? Did he know the girl? Did he understand the circumstances of the case?

"I don't mind saying that I know the girl intimately, and that I should be very pleased to make any little discovery I could about her."

"Ay," said Leslie; and as they approached a swampy margin to the river, over which they had to get by hop-step-and-leap, the conversation stopped for a time.

"I wonder at a young man like you," commenced Leslie, with all his own manner restored to him, "taking up with a foolish notion of finding gold, when you have a profession to make your way upon. They tell me you are an advocate—an advocate! and you came north on our mail-coach to riddle dirt, hoping to find what would remunerate you for your trouble. Why, man, from every point of view it's the behaviour of an idiot."

"I was led to believe that you had faith in the supply. Indeed, since I came here I have seen or heard something of a company starting to work the ore. What's idiotic about my doing for myself what a company is doing for the excellent British public?"

"I think you are about as simple a character as the shepherd who first brought me the intelligence."

"Oliver Gun ?"

Again Leslie looked as if he were ill.

Nixon remarked the change in his face, and disliked his symptoms; they seemed to indicate so much personal hostility to himself. But he offered him his sympathy, which was accepted without words. When he had quite recovered, and looked less like a man longing to commit a murderous assault, Nixon asked him—

"Is there anything peculiarly simple about the shepherd ?"

"We have nothing to do with the shepherd," said the other. "But I see you, a young man, throwing away your opportunities—your brilliant opportunities—of making your name and your fame at the bar, and coming away up here, a small fishing station on a cold coast, with no opportunities of fortune for any, and establishing yourself at work which can only last but a brief period. Go back, man, to your Parliament House, and take up the gown you have cast off. You are nothing but a waif and a vagabond hĕre ; there you are no worse than scores of others, even if you are badly off for money. Don't I know ? Haven't I supplied the courts with more cases than any factor out of the north, and haven't I the experience requisite for advising you ?"

"It's very good of you, Mr. Leslie, to take such a fatherly interest in me—very good, I'm sure; and I would be indebted to you if I could understand your rapid alterations of manner, from one which looks like a savage intention to assault me, to another which patronizes me with as much affection as if I belonged to you. I quite appreciate all you say about the Parliament House, but you will allow me to know the details of my own life better than you. I don't stand in need of advice. Heaven knows, I've had enough of advice in my day to establish a college of sages in a good going business. But my experience of it is, that it is about as permanently useful as a pinch of snuff, and a hanged deal more aggravating at the time."

"A young man knows everything," said Leslie. "Positively everything. Give him five-and-twenty years—I suppose that's about your spell—and there's nothing in heaven or earth, or behind the veil, that he doesn't know as well as the Creator Himself."

"No; I make no pretensions to omniscience."

"That's well. It's a wise man, they say, that knows his own father."

It was now Nixon's turn to start and look a little ill.

"My sagacity," he said bitterly, "ends at my father. I don't know him. I never knew him. If I knew him I should not be standing on the edge of this bitter moor looking into the Rudder with you."

"Come, come," said Leslie, with a touch of softness in his voice. "This alters the case. Then you have no subsistence at the bar. You are without funds, you are without friends, you are a waif and without briefs. Now look at me, Mr. Nixon. I command a considerable field of law. I can see that briefs are sent you. Back you go to Edinburgh and you will have business."

"Ah! I have known such jolly fellows in the country over their tenth tumbler make me just such promises. But—but Mr. Leslie, the business never came. The jolly promisers forgot all about it when I was out of sight. Excuse me if I am a little sceptical."

Again a fit of illness overtook Mr. Leslie. Nixon turned aside from the footpath in case he should be leant upon. Then of a sudden, with the force of an explosion, Leslie burst out:

"Then, curse you, what are you here for? Are you here to spy upon me? Are you here from the Court of Session? But you'll find you're dealing with the wrong man for once."

An apoplectic flush rushed over his face, and he stopped for words.

"You are giving yourself a quantity of unnecessary trouble about me, Mr. Leslie. I've been everywhere over Scotland, and no man ever stopped to ask me *why* I was here or there—no man until I have come across you. Keep your mind easy. I am not here to spy upon you."

"What have you got to do with Mina Durie?" he burst out. "Isn't she well enough under a good man's protection? Can't you let well alone? Why, man, she may be a fish-brat, for aught you know. Isn't she better to remain as she is than revert to that through over-curiosity? Go back, man, to Parliament House and practise your profession."

"We're not hitting it off, Mr. Leslie; good-evening. You will allow me to mind my own business."

Nixon returned to the town, but Leslie leant up against a cairn of stones and looked towards the mountains. A far time came back to his memory, a time of youth and lawlessness which he thought he had buried for ever. But no, the dead past was yielding up ghosts to menace him. His respecta-

bility, his hold over Ruddersdale, his very liberty
to go and come, were all threatened. His life seemed
tumbling in ruins about his ears. But, by heaven!
he would make a fight of it. He would not be
driven from place and power at the nod of the first
birkie who came out of the south. Birkie must be
less inquisitive, or——Again Mr. Leslie of Ruddersdale looked exceedingly ill.

CHAPTER XV.

UP THE MOUNTAIN.

Nixon had never paid a visit to Cnoc Dhu so as to reach the summit. It was a peculiarity of his that when in the neighbourhood of mountains, or, indeed, of anything shooting into the air, he always longed to be on the top, and it was only a question of time with him when he should reach it. He set aside a day for himself to get up Cnoc Dhu, that he might the better understand the strange land into which he had fallen. The day after his talk with Leslie he had nothing better to do than resume his exploration. There was the mountain, and there was—yes, there was the girl by the way, he had met on Loch Dirlot. He shouldn't in the least mind seeing her again. He would rather like to see her. His short engagement with Mina had given him a glimpse into the charm of companionship with women who were capable of affection. He did not care for this girl's affection in the least. A shepherd's daughter on the mountains! All he should care about was the suggestion she should make of another love for another. If he were vicariously reminded, that was enough for him. Perhaps he would not have thought of her at all in connection with Cnoc Dhu, had he not mentioned to Nancy Harper that on the island beyond the mountain he had lighted upon a Highland young lady who had once occupied the same room as he was now in himself.

"You're jokin', sir," said Nancy. "There's nobody goes on that loch from year's end to year's end, but Duncan Elder and Oliver Gun—and, maybe, Elspeth."

"Very well, Mrs. Harper, it was just Elspeth I met there. Believe me, Elspeth is what they would consider a beauty in the south. I don't know what they consider her here, there are so many pretty female faces though none quite like Elspeth's. She has so much dignity of carriage, so much reserve of grace, and such an attractive shyness."

"Poor lassie!" said Mrs. Harper with emotion; "I'm fonder o' Elspeth than of ony lassie ever lived. I cannot say what my own would have turned oot had she lived. Ay, ay—weel, weel—God knows best; it was for my sins she was removed!"

"That's not how things happen, Mrs. Harper. I know one of the wickedest sinners on earth, who has broken nearly every law in the Decalogue, and he has a family of the most beautiful daughters."

"Aweel, they've been made daughters instead o' sons for his sins."

"There's no arguing with you. There are some funny anomalies in the world."

"Aweel, I've seen an ill-faured tree loaded with fine fruit in autumn. But that Elspeth, she just beats everything I ever saw; the e'en that she has when she's standin' at that window, lookin' oot ower the sea. She'll say, 'That's a big, big ship yonder, Nancy.' She ca's me Nancy, puir thing, tho' I've a weel-kent-hoose, and she's but a shepherd's daughter. She'll say, 'That's a big ship,' an' no ship to be seen. An' I'll say, 'Hoot awa wi' your nonsense, lassie ; it's you that disna ken the sea and the white faem o't, an' the drivin' cloods, and the trails o' snawy mist. There's nae sail there ava'.' And she'll stick till't, an' say, 'Nancy, it's a big ship, forby the smacks in the harbour. I can count the sails.' An' a pilot-body or a fisherman will come in, an' they'll say, 'Ship, ship —ay, there's a ship; a clipper comin' roond wi' timber frae Quebec, maist likely for Leith.' Now, she's richt efter a', ye see. Oh, sic an e'e, and sic a han' an' airm, an' fit, an' middle. Eh, Elspeth's just the perfection o' a lass for a young man's fancy."

"Yes, she's a wonderful product of the mountains," said Nixon. "I'm going up that way. Will I say that you sent your love to her?"

"Ay, ay, do that, Mr. Nixon. Ye micht, if ye have room in your pack, put in a bit book o' sangs out o' the sooth. Elspeth can read, and her father's a great man for a book, if he can come by it without too much expense. No, I'll no' put bannocks in your pack, for they go all to meal. You're safer wi' loaf-breed an' twa-three cauld cuts o' troot, wi' your flask. Coming, coming!"

Nixon set out for Cnoc Dhu from the high crags to the north of Ruddersdale, and came round upon the base of the mountain above the shepherd's house. He looked for the shieling for a long time without finding it. It was as difficult to find as a wren's nest in a bank of clay: nothing more cunning than a wren at building and concealing her large mansion of moss and feathers. A shepherd's shieling in a mountain swept by the storms of the north, is as craftily disposed to elude inspection. At last, however, Nixon came upon it, by following the burn where the gold had been first discovered. He had not been there before; he noted how neatly everything was disposed beneath the shelving cliff—the stack of peats to the side of the shieling, the flower-pots in the windows, the whitewash of the walls, the ash-tree hedge of the little garden, one of the trees containing the large nest of a magpie, the overflow of the burn carried by a pipe into a rocky basin—everything struck him as cleanly, healthy, pretty. As he stepped down the hewn side of the dusky cliff above the house, the shepherd's wife came out and looked at him. She had seen him from a side window. She had not many visitors at the shieling; and as she had years ago given up visiting Ruddersdale, she was not very familiar with faces.

"You will be Mrs. Gun," said Nixon. "I came along from Ruddersdale, rowed up the Cranberry burn as far as it runs, and walked across the moors. I'm rather wet about the feet and legs. I thought I would come in on you and ask a few questions about Cnoc Dhu."

"Surely, surely, sir," said Mrs. Gun. "Come your ways in, sir, and sit down. Elspeth, come, here's a gentleman from Ruddersdale. You'll be from the bank ?"

Elspeth came to the door, drying her hands, and, to her mother's surprise, she exclaimed:—

"Oh, it's you, is it? And are you very well, indeed? I met him, mother, on the island of Dirlot. Father knows him too."

"You'll be hungry after your walk," said Mrs. Gun.

"Yes, rather. But Nancy Harper put some kippers into my pack, and I haven't eaten them yet. If you'll give me the use of a chair, I'll sit and eat under your roof-tree."

"Surely," said Mrs. Gun, who did not dislike the look of the youth. "Elspeth, lay the cloth."

They laid it, and Nixon began to eat.

"The shepherd's up the mountain," said his wife to one of his inquiries. "You see he has to follow the sheep, and they're very keen to get their feed high up when the weather breaks. No, no, he never loses any of them. What would he lose his sheep for? Dear me, a sheep's not a silly animal at all. You're very far wrong to think the like o' that. Don't they all know Cnoc Dhu, every sheep o' them? And don't they know their own lee corners and their own craig tops? Surely, sir, as well as you know your own home in the south. We had an old tup, we used to call him Roderick, after Mr. Leslie, and no disrespect to him whatever. Well, he was sold away over the mountains to a man who keeps a farm on the West. We was very sorry to part with Roderick, for he came a great deal about the shieling. But what does he do? He walks across the mountains a week after he was sold—ay, a hundred miles and more; and Oliver, he says, ''Deed, I'll never say a word about it. The poor tup can just bide where he is.' And there he is to this hour."

"I'm anxious to get to the top of Cnoc Dhu to-day," said Nixon. "Do you think the shepherd could go up with me?"

"Well, Elspeth, you can take the gentleman up as far as your father is; but I wouldn't say that the mist isn't on the summit, and if that's the case, you'll not win farther than the bottom of the crags. Surely, lassie, you can go up if you like. Take the gentleman round by the view above Dirlot, and show him the birds flying above the islands."

Elspeth and Nixon ascended the steps above the shieling together, and got on to a broad tableland of moor.

"It's very pleasant to see you so soon again," said Elspeth when they had started together. "That's Roderick there, see, the old tup that my mother was talking about. He doesn't go very far away from the house now. He's getting an aged tup."

"What an old formidable blackguard! He has a face as black as black. His horns are like antlers."

"Oh, Roderick can beat any tup on the mountain, but he's tired of it. See, he's away to the back of that big rock to get the lee. He knows you're a stranger. Now, we'll begin to go straight up till we get on the crags overlooking Dirlot. I'll go before you and show you the way. I'll not go very fast, because it'll take the wind from you, and that's not good. We'll find my father somewhere about there. He's counting the lambs to-day. They're very fine, strong, healthy lambs the year."

"I say, you certainly have a magnificent pair of lungs. I consider myself rather a mountaineer, but I can't address myself to the face of a steep ridge, exactly as if it were a level road. Hold on a little ! I must turn and look back."

"Sit down, then, and look about you, and I'll wait. But you lose your wind very soon."

He sat down on a loose rock. Elspeth with her knuckles in her sides, stood above him, looking back too. They saw over a broad expanse of moorland.

Indeed there was nothing but a long brown undulation of moor, dipping here and there into a valley with a glistening stream, rising into a lesser mountain than Cnoc Dhu—undulating and dipping mile upon mile, until, as it seemed, there was a fringe like the sea in the horizon. He asked if it were the sea.

"No, not yet," said Elspeth: "higher up, on the very top of Cnoc Dhu, we can see the sea; not so low down as this. That's blue sky. Indeed, I don't know if it's sky at all. It's blue distance I think."

Nixon rose from his stone, and Elspeth set off in front of him, springing lightly from ridge to ridge, throwing back speech at him as she ascended, encouraging him amidst difficulties, laughing at his halts, and, finally helping him with a strong right arm to the rocky plateau which overlooked Dirlot loch, where they had first met.

"I thought I could climb," said Nixon; "now I know that I've got to learn the art. You run up a mountain."

"Don't I belong to Cnoc Dhu? Isn't it as well known to me as to these?" pointing to a group of sheep nibbling roots, while some hardy young lambs leapt in the air and made eccentric spiral motions with their legs.

"True, but they are lambs, and you are——"

"Here's my father."

"I took you for the Duke of Burrows, sir," said the shepherd, coming down from behind a blind of turf, where he appeared to have been dozing; "he sometimes comes up Cnoc Dhu. We're not to look at him if he comes. We're not even to lift a hat to him. If we do, we're dismissed on the spot, if we're on the Burrows property. You a little resemble him, sir. Have you any business on the mountain, wi' the sheep like, or the ferns, or the geology, or the—heh! heh!—the goold?"

"Not much, Mr. Gun, of that sort. Only I am trying to bring back to the memory of old inhabitants a period when a ship came ashore and a babe was carried from it to Roderick Leslie's house. Do you happen to remember that period ?"

The shepherd took out his crook from beneath his left elbow, planted it firmly on the ground, seemed to lean on it heavily, gazed into the horizon, evading meanwhile the gaze of his interlocutor; then, with a slightly lowering look as he gathered his plaid about him, replied—

"Are you personally interested in the finding of the child ? Is it your business to find her ? Has Sir—I mean, has anything been heard of her father ? Am I at liberty to answer you with perfect freedom, as a man giving his opinion of his recollections, without any use being made of them ?"

The shepherd seemed to remember more than anybody Nixon had questioned. Nixon recollected that he was himself a lawyer.

"Shepherd," he said, "if you know anything of that child and the circumstances of her delivery into the hand of Roderick Leslie, tell me. I am engaged in the law. I will see that you are rewarded for speaking the truth."

The shepherd looked at Elspeth, who on a distant margin of the cliff was looking down on Dirlot, and replied—

"Come down to my house, and I'll give you my notion."

CHAPTER XVI.

USHER'S TURN.

POVERTY is not the best bride for ambition, though it is the bride to which ambition is often enough temporarily wedded. In Frank Usher's case it assorted badly with his entire plans of life. He was as ambitious as it is possible for a young man to be. He saw himself toiling through a period of years of cheap briefs, and reaching a point when he might be as fastidious as he chose. He looked forward to a day when he should head his faculty and go into Parliament. He saw himself come out of Parliament to ascend the Bench, and in that dignified retiral expound the laws of his country. In the glory of titled neutrality known as paper lordship he would have realized all the happiness which he believed life possessed. In the meantime, however, to keep himself in his modest state of apparent independence, he must set his hands to what he would have been spared had he been born rich. He must, for example, draw up a prospectus for a stockbroker, setting forth that gold was to be found at the Marnock Firth. Had it been anything but gold he would have gone to work on his prospectus with the assurance of ignorance. If it had been a company for the extraction of whale-oil, or for the compression of peats, or the collection in unparalleled quantities of herrings, he would have drawn it with enthusiasm. But gold ! However, he swallowed his scruples, drew out the prospectus, leaving blanks for his friend the stockbroker to fill up when there were figures to insert. It was one of the things he would rather not have done. He did it believing that the sooner he got through the muddier necessities of his profession the earlier should he begin to wade in clear water. The question of Mina Durie's heritage, which he had raised at Durie Den, weighed on his mind a good deal in those days. He had seen Leslie's response to the languid inquiries of the sheriff, and his summary to himself of the situation was: " Old fogeys! Can't be bothered investigating. Quite satisfied with things as they are. Sheriff can't think of dropping his ward, now that she is permanently established at his fireside. But old fogeydom must be disturbed. Justice will have to be done. If the girl be Mina Dunbeath! By Jove!—if she be, and I am the heaven-appointed advocate who is to take up her brief! What a case! Plead her cause, and marry her! I wish wives gave their titles to their husbands, though. Let me see, how does it sound? Lady Dunbeath and Mr. Frank Usher: no—is a baronet's daughter, a ladyship? I think not. But it would not be so suspicious-looking, after I had ascended the Bench and travelled with her in foreign hotels, as signing myself Lord Usher, while she signed herself plain Mrs. Usher. And I am to meet her and the

Finlays to-day at the Picture Gallery. Lady Dunbeath—yes, I have a correct presentiment that she is the heir."

He had an appointment that day to meet Mina and her friends, Gerty and Bessie Finlay, at the door of the National Gallery. "Poor Nixon!" he thought; "he is out of it—no hope for him now." And perhaps there was some truth in the reflection; for Mina, though she had pledged herself to Nixon, was not beyond reach of the opinion of her friends. She had heard what they thought, how they regarded Nixon as, on the whole, a poor creature who was not of much consideration. She knew that the sheriff regarded him in the same light, while she saw that Usher had all his approbation. In the first instance it had turned her heart more towards Nixon. She had gone up to the hollow tree, and wept in it for a good hour at a time, and called him her knight and her true love, and said to herself that she would die for him or live only till he had succeeded in his search, or searching, come back to tell her that he had done his best and she was now his.

Usher stood on the steps of the Royal Academy when the sheriff's carriage drove up. The sheriff was not in it; only the three girls. Gerty and Bessie were very glad to have the opportunity of meeting Usher. They had met him before, and were not without a latent hope that the brilliant rising advocate might cast an eye of appreciation on one or other of them.

"Dearest Mina," Gerty had said on the way to the Academy, "it's so good of you to give us a chance of meeting him."

"Dearest Gerty," Mina had said, "you are welcome to him."

"If our noses were only different!" said Bessie.

Usher stepped down, hat in hand, as if the gallery were his own, and he were introducing some friends into it. The girls were quite pleased at their chaperon. He looked distinguished, though his face was pale—distinguished, with the fire of intellect in his eye. Gerty and Bessie both thought they would engage themselves to him at the first asking, if he only advanced that far.

"Everybody says it's a first-rate exhibition," said Usher, addressing Mina, and leading the way to the wicket. He bought three catalogues, handed them round, and taking possession of Mina, began generalizing. Bessie and Gerty were disappointed : he seemed to be conscious only of Mina's presence.

"There's not much in the North Octagon," he began, " but enough, as you may see in a glance, to show that they have had foul weather for their work."

"How do you mean?" said Gerty, determined that she at least was not to be ignored at the side of an engaged girl.

" I mean that when the artists go out and find their mountains, rocks, and bays enveloped in mist, they bring back their weather with them. Observe how from floor to roof the gallery is filled with pictures of mist. I don't think it's fair of them. Mist and mystery are all very well in poetry and descriptive prose, but when you come to having it on canvas it looks to me like men shirking their work."

"Bessie dear," said Gerty, "did you know that Bobby Bertram had a picture in the gallery? He is numbered 1065 in my catalogue. That's very mischievous of Bobby; he never said anything about it; he is ever so much cleverer than I thought he was."

"To my mind," pursued Usher, still addressing Mina, "there's only one picture in the North Octagon."

"Which one?"

"Loch Dirlot."

"No. 5?"

"It has, for one thing, been taken without mist, and that shoulder of mountain stands up as solid as any granite crag I ever saw. You could almost put your hands on the lower shelves and climb up. Come back a little way and look at it. Never mind that old man stooping at it, and showing us an ungainly back view of himself. What a tiresome old donkey !"

They waited for a little until the individual who presented the back view should go away, but he showed no signs of caring to depart.

" I say, my good man," remarked Usher, advancing to him, putting his hand upon his shoulder, and with a high patronizing voice exclaiming, "you ought to remember there are more people in the North Octagon than you. That picture was painted for the public, I believe."

The girls tittered, but the individual declined to move; when he did turn, however, Usher instantaneously doffed his hat, and exclaimed, "I beg pardon, m' lud ; I had no idea it was you."

"It's not a picture at all," said my lord, presenting to the group a face in which a pair of keen searching eyes looked over a massive unshaped nose, beneath which the jaws had the aspect of nut-crackers.

"No," said Usher, recalling his previous opinion with instantaneous promptitude, "I agree with you. I think the harmony of water and sky is outraged, and the rock is ——"

"It's otherwise interesting," said his lordship, "from the circumstance that it is from these shores we are going to supply the mint in the future."

And his lordship emitted a low chuckle. He put up a *pince-nez,* and turning a searching eye upon Mina, he said:

"I seem to have some recollection of your face."

"Miss Durie—Lord Straven," said the advocate, "Lord Straven—the Misses Finlay."

Mina recoiled, for it was the judge who had snubbed Joseph ; but Gerty and Bessie came forward and shook hands with the old man.

"What does the sheriff think of the exhibition, Miss Durie ? "

"He hasn't been yet, my lord."

"I'm afraid he's occupying too much of his time

with his 'Eminent Scotch Sheriffs.'" And again my lord emitted a chuckle, not so low as the previous one. "Never mind me," he added, waving them unceremoniously into the Great Room; "I take my own time to look at them, and though I recognize, Mr. Usher, that pictures are painted for the public, I'm not going to deny myself the privilege of examining them at close quarters, and in an attitude which may be less dignified than is befitting one of Her Majesty's judges, because that attitude may not be the one you choose to adopt, accompanied as you are by these young ladies. Good-day, good-day." And he returned to his dorsal manner, to the amusement of Gerty, who stuffed her handkerchief in her mouth to prevent herself laughing.

But Usher looked very serious, and interrupted the fit of giggling by the remark, "He is a magnificent critic of pictures. He has made a noble collection in his house, and there is no one whose opinion is so much sought after by artists. I wish I hadn't patronized him. I'll get it hot for that some fine afternoon when I'm pleading at my best in the Outer House."

They were now well into the Great Room. There was a crowd in it.

"Oh lovely!" burst out Gerty, seeing imitable dresses to the right and left of her.

"Gerty, have more self-restraint," whispered Bessie, while Usher and Mina stood apart.

Mina was thinking of the judge's remark about the mint, and wondering whether Loch Dirlot had anything to do with Joseph. Usher was murmuring that "art was long and life was short."

And, indeed, the entrance into the Great Room was calculated to impress any observer. How the invisible workers had wandered into the land of the Beautiful, and what spoil they had brought back! They had gone into the glens, and brought back mountains; they had gone down to the sea in ships, and mirrored the billows breaking on the headlands;

they had stood by the rivers, and rendered their pools and their waterfalls as Nature might be proud to render them; they had searched the harbours, and carried away quaint Dutch faces and sea-beaten expressions. From the market-place they had taken women chaffering; from the fields men ploughing, girls milking, boys herding; they had set down baskets of fruit ripe and lush, flowers and leaves in the perfection of their shape. There were lithe maidens from southern climes; other skies hung over them than Scotland boasted; other sunrises and sunsets lay dreaming on the canvas; springs which strewed the world with unknown herbage; summers which brought strange languor upon the land; and autumns whose fruits were the grape, the orange, and the pomegranate.

"I can take my hat off here, Miss Durie," said the advocate, "and carry it under my arm. The men to whom we decree neglect and vagabondage do all that."

Gerty had disappeared, and at that moment returned.

"I've seen Bobby Bertram's picture. Such a thing as *it* is! Right out of sight at the top of the North Room. You never saw anything so perfectly hideous. Two pigs in a sty, and they haven't the shape of pigs either. I'll never speak to Bobby again for doing anything so hideous."

Nobody listened to Gerty, however, though her indignation seemed to cause some amusement to the bystanders who didn't know her.

Bessie only looked at her, to remark—

"Well, really, Gerty, to be an engaged girl, Mina is looking very queer at Mr. Usher."

"Yes, indeed. One would suppose that there wasn't such a person as Mr. Nixon at all. Mina," added Gerty, breaking in upon the apparent sentimentalism of aspect of the pair, "what did that old man mean about the mint? What did he mean Mr. Usher?"

"I didn't quite take him," said the advocate, who understood perfectly what he meant, but saw no reason why Joseph should be flaunted under the eye of Miss Durie; for they advanced into the South Octagon, and towards the South Room they met common friends, who broke up the party for a little, though Usher kept his attention fixed upon Mina. She had been exchanging remarks for a time with some one from the Castle, who twirled a heavy moustache heavily; and some other one from Jock's Lodge, who made the bystanders aware that he was wearing spurs. Then she rapidly left them, and turned into a room called the Small Octagon. She was standing by herself, in front of a picture of two lovers bidding each other good-bye between a hedge of roses. He had obviously only done kissing her, and the premonitory symptoms of departure were strong in the gathering sorrow of her brow and the tearful expression of her eyes.

"They have given it a wretched bad light, and put

it into the condemned cell," said Usher softly. "But I think there is a great deal of feeling in it; and the hedge-roses, which might have been spoilt by garishness, retain all the charms of the roses with a perfect restraint in the ruddier tones. I think the heroine of the picture is not unlike you, Miss Durie."

Mina started visibly, and dropping her voice, as she looked towards the door, through which no one entered:

"Curious that I should have been thinking that the—hero was not unlike Mr. Frank Usher. I see no resemblance to myself. To you I can trace a distinct and happy likeness; only I should say the departing lover is a soldier, and not a lawyer."

"Yes, you are right; I think he is probably an army man. I wonder how it is that we poor fellows who have to deal with parchments, and whose hearts are quite as susceptible beneath stuff or silk as soldiers under uniform, are so seldom put into canvas in appropriately affectionate attitudes."

"You are all so—so practical and——"

"And love demands the impracticable, the unreal, the—— ? "

"I don't know what it is," said Mina, "but it would look odd, wouldn't it? to see old Lord Straven making love in a lane, or the Lord Justice Clerk on his knees to some hard-hearted beauty who was spurning him; or the Lord President marching off to the altar, with the Lord Advocate or the Solicitor-General acting as his groomsman. Somehow, it would not be so curious if a General were to do the same thing."

"You take the same view as the artist," sighed Usher; "and yet we lawyers all marry wives, and wives are not to be won without a little courtship among the roses."

Mina turned her eyes full upon him. Her face wore its most mischievous expression at the moment. He saw that he had not touched her heart, but that he had interested her.

"I am in earnest," he said; and the mischievous light in her eyes died out of them.

"Oh, here you are, are you? I thought I should pick you up somewhere," said a voice from the door.

It was the sheriff, and Mina breathed freely as she turned round to greet him.

"Usher, did you happen to see Straven drifting up the room? Do you know what he says about Smeaton's fairies,—that waterside picture in the second room, you know, with the incomplete elves and fairies ducking and bobbing among the leaves? You saw it, Mina? Yes. Well, go into a corner and turn your back till I tell Frank what Straven said."

"Eh—what? I didn't catch it," observed Usher eagerly.

"That there was an inartistic absence of haunches among them," whispered the sheriff.

"Papa dear, if you please," said Mina, "you will find me in the other room."

"And it's a fact," said the sheriff, looking contemptuously at the lovers in the lane.

CHAPTER XVII.

A MEAL.

Oliver Gun paused on the descent and gathered his faculties together. "Like John Anderson and his jo," he said after a little, "Elspeth and you can gang doun the hill thegither. I'll be at your back in a wee." The shepherd was afraid that in promising to give the stranger his "notion," he was deeply committing himself. He paused, therefore, to get his full stock of caution, and to bethink himself how he might say the least about the subject to which the stranger had alluded.

"I should like to stand for a quarter of an hour or so, overlooking Dirlot," said Nixon; "there's nothing puts my spirits up like a high wind. It's an occasion I always rise to. And there's something about this wind that speaks for itself of the North Sea and the frosted pole beyond all."

"Your spirits would never be down, then, on this mountain," said the shepherd. "Elspeth 'll show you anything you want pointed out to you. I'll away to my lambs for a wee. If you're not here when I come back, I'll know that you have gone down to the house."

The pair stood looking over the plain of ruffled water. The wind blew Elspeth's sun-hat over her shoulders and her hair broke loose. Nixon helped her to capture it again, and to imprison it within the sun-hat.

"There's nobody ever helped me to do that before," said the girl. "Is that the way the girls in the south——Oh, I'm just speaking foolish nonsense."

"When they are nice," said Nixon, believing that he understood what she had intended to say.

Elspeth looked over her shoulder towards the

retreating figure of her father. When Nixon next glanced at her, he perceived that her grey eyes were wistfully fastened upon him.

"Now, don't you get tired of this," he asked, "from year's end to year's end? Of course, I'm not going to disparage it. To me it's earthly paradise. But *all* the year round, you know?"

"Never," said Elspeth. "Maybe I will when I come to grow older." And a sigh went off on the breeze which Nixon did not hear.

"I can't think what you find to do for twelve months on end—four of them at least under snow."

"That's what some of them think down in Ruddersdale town, who know no better. Nancy Harper has said the same to me—and others. But if you knew the changes that come over Cnoc Dhu—if you knew that one month is always different from another month, that the heather on the hill is different, the animals that run on it and the birds that fly over it different, the very burn different — you wouldn't think as you do."

"You seem to have quite a personal feeling of championship about your old hill."

"It's not a hill at all; it's a mountain—the very loftiest of all the mountains. There's no other that approaches it in magnificence. I have a book at home where the person who saw it and printed about it said no other approaches it in magnificence."

"You are quite in love with old Cnoc Dhu. He's a respectable size of a lover to have."

"I don't know anything about these things. But as father was saying, we may as well gang doun the hill together. I'll only allow you to call Cnoc Dhu a hill when you are speaking out of an old song."

"Well, well, mountain be it," and they began to descend.

Nixon waited for an hour or more in the shieling. Elspeth gave him her father's fly-book to examine, and his comments showed the girl that he knew what he was talking about. He knew all about sea-trout and loch-trout; about smoults, and parr, and salmon, how they came and went; how they were born, brought up, persecuted by the otters and the birds, till they ended their lives, after a noble struggle, in the angler's basket. She showed him her father's Brown Bess, too, and was a little disconcerted when he pronounced it rather old-fashioned, and wondered how anybody could shoot anything with it.

"But I suppose Mr. Gun doesn't shoot much? I thought, in fact, that shepherds were not allowed to have guns at all."

"And there you are right enough, too," said the shepherd's wife, looking at Elspeth with some anxiety.

"Ay, but my father's not like any other shepherd. Mr. Leslie never would refuse him the use of his gun. What do you think would happen if the mountain foxes were to be allowed to have it all their own way, and to take a lamb or a fowl whenever they liked? Many's the fox that gun has sent to his long home."

"He has shot eagles, too," said Mrs. Gun. "There's nothing he cannot shoot, if Mr. Leslie will but allow him."

"Then, indeed, you needn't be so dull as I supposed."

"We're not dull at all," said Mrs. Gun, with a renewal of anxiety, and looking towards Elspeth, who glanced at her and said—

"I wasn't complaining, mother."

The shepherd having corked himself up to his satisfaction, came down from Cnoc Dhu. It was such an unusual thing for a stranger to call and make inquiries, and concerning a date so far back as eighteen years. It was a new thing in his experience. He had indeed heard, the last time he was in Ruddersdale, that strange things were occurring in the south, which might ultimately affect Mr. Leslie and the Ruddersdale property from the Cnoc Dhu to the sea. He had not, however, given much attention to the rumour; it was enough for him that Roderick Leslie was standing in his bank-parlour as large as life, which in this case was exceedingly large, round, and vital. Cnoc Dhu might crumble, thought the shepherd, but Roderick Leslie could not be imagined out of his bank-parlour, or away from the valley of Sir Thomas Dunbeath's river.

"That's father come down the mountain now," said Elspeth, as his figure momentarily darkened the little casement of the shieling.

"You were longer than you said you would be, father."

"Were you thinking it long, sir?"

"Not a bit of it, Mr. Gun. It would be a poor compliment to your wife and daughter if I were to weary after less than an hour of their company."

"People from the south," observed Mrs. Gun, "say things in a very nice way. It's a long time before you would say the like o' that to Elspeth and me, Oliver."

"It is the eddication," remarked Oliver. "I notice that the eddication is a great advantage to a person in saying a thing nicely. I would be looking about me and scratching my head and thinking about it all the time, and the nice thing would occur to me half an hour afterwards, when it's not of any use."

"Oh, a compliment's never thrown away, Oliver Gun."

"Be thankful wi' what you have got, Christina," said the shepherd.

Mrs. Gun set down a meal for the stranger. Tea was her great luxury. Tea she made, therefore, and with what she called "crowdy" in a bowl, and warm scones, and large eggs, and white rolls of butter, and an incisive appetite on Nixon's part, he did nearly as well as the shepherd, who having asked a blessing, which rather cooled the tea, so long was it, put away vast quantities of everything in the most limited space of time.

"We were talking up the hill," said Nixon, "about an incident which occurred."

The shepherd saw that his "notion" was to be broached; his mouth was full at the moment, but he interrupted Nixon vehemently with a sound like "No-a-hiy."

"A mountain, sir, if you please," said Mrs. Gun. "Not a hill, Oliver's saying. Oliver, speak when you've swallowed your bite, man; the gentleman 'll no be accustomed to that sort of way of going on in the south."

"Oh yes, Mrs. Gun, I've seen a man in the south with his mouth full, talking away. But, to be sure, nobody understood him but himself. We settled that by the way—didn't we, Miss Gun?—that Cnoc Dhu is not a hill, but a mountain."

"No other approaches it in magnificence," said Elspeth.

" No, nor in kind hospitality," added Nixon, chipping a fresh egg. " However," he continued, " to go back upon what we were saying higher up. There was a wreck in Marnock Bay something like eighteen years ago."

Oliver bolted a large " bite " with great expedition.

"Is that all you know, sir? A wreck! Ae wreck! One wreck in eighteen years! There's a score o' ships ashore round and round the Marnock Firth every winter. There's been that within the living memory of man."

"You're only interrupting the gentleman, Oliver. He wants to put a question to you."

The shepherd opened his jaws, and above his beard revealed a set of teeth as white as the collies' which were sitting near the elbows of the company in a contemplative attitude.

"Now, you're angry, father," said Elspeth, "about nothing."

"No, I'm not angry, Christina Gun—very far from

it. I'm not one who is given to useless puffs o' wind. But ye know as well as I do that the Bay of Marnock is very little known to me—that I am very much of a stranger in the Bay of Marnock, that the ships which have come ashore there, and the lives saved and the lives lost, are as little known to me as to the lassie."

He spoke with strong emphasis, and his eyes were fixed upon his wife's face with so strong a glance of repression that Nixon inwardly remarked, "This man knows something I ought to know."

"You remember, however, I suppose, Mr. Gun—in fact, everybody remembers: I speak to nobody who doesn't—you remember that there was a little girl brought ashore, of whom Roderick Leslie took charge?"

"I cannot charge my memory with it, sir," said the shepherd, moving uneasily in his chair, pushing that bit of furniture back upon one of the dogs, who howled, and inserting two fingers into his vest pocket, from which he took out a short cutty pipe.

"Down in Ruddersdale," said Nixon, "everybody I talk to has some recollection of the circumstance."

"Ay, you see, but we're twenty miles from the ocean here—twenty long heather miles."

"Have you any interest in the bit lassie?" asked Mrs. Gun.

"The deepest interest in life," said Nixon, "she's my sweetheart. I've come up here to discover all I can about her. When I know how she came to be on your coast eighteen years ago, I shall be entitled to say to her, 'Now, be my wife.'"

Mrs. Gun seemed alarmed. A shade of depression stole into Elspeth's face : she asked, almost tearfully, "And do you think you will be long in finding her?"

"Who can tell?"

"I would like to give you a helping hand."

"And I'll take it gladly."

"It's a queer story," said Oliver Gun.

"You're a real enterprising gentleman," said Mrs. Gun, with an admiring accent to her voice.

"We'll be seeing some more of you, if it's your sweetheart you're after; she was here, and doesn't know how."

"I'm here for another reason, too; I'm going to dig for gold one of these days."

"Well, then," said Elspeth with an exclamation of delight, "I would be very glad to help you at it."

"The gentleman's only joking," said the smoking Oliver. "I doubt if Elspeth hasn't got all the gold there is, sir."

"Where there was a little, there will be more."

"I'm not taken up with the notion of it," said Mrs. Gun.

"Down in Ruddersdale they are making preparations for any quantity of it."

"To think of the like of that!"

By-and-by Nixon rose, thanked his hosts for their kindness to him, and offered to pay for his meal, which greatly shocked them.

"Nobody ever paid for a meal in this house," said Oliver with much dignity. "Nobody ever will."

"I am sorry I offered it. Good-bye, all of you."

He ascended the cliff above the shieling and got on to the moorland again. The new season's lapwings were wheeling over it and shrieking. They had not been there all winter. They regarded Nixon's solitary figure with noisy suspicion. As he pursued his way, a full half hour from the shieling he heard the panting of breath behind him. He turned and fronted Elspeth.

"Maybe I'm doing wrong," she said; "but I couldn't think of you looking for your sweetheart without telling you that Nancy Harper said to me once about the girl, 'Wha kens, lassie, maybe she never was aboard the ship.'"

CHAPTER XVIII.

THERE were times when Joseph Nixon, thinking of his own origin, wandered back from the world of present reality into chaos. The fact that he had no father or mother known to him, and never had, turned him into a metaphysician. The "Who am I ?" in relation to a physical father and a physical mother, which got no answer, threw him back to the "Who am I ?" in relation to the whole mystery of life. As he watched the comely figure of Elspeth Gun, retreating towards the shieling, after throwing at him an enigmatical word about his sweetheart, he resumed his way across the moor, murmuring a passage from an English writer, which had sunk deep into his mind: "Earth's mountains are levelled, and her seas filled up, in our passage; can the earth, which is but dead and a vision, resist spirits which have reality and are alive? On the hardest adamant, some footprint of us is stamped in; the last rear of the host will read traces of the earliest van. But whence? Oh, Heaven! whither? Sense knows not; Faith knows not." He repeated the passage over and over again to himself as he swept across the moor, blackening under the stars, until he regained his hidden canoe at the head of the Cranberry Burn. He got into it, paddle in hand, and for a long time he did not touch the face of the stream. He allowed himself to drift downwards with the running water. How it sang to him, as he descended, little lullabies which seemed to speak of forgotten voices in other spheres, notes of rush and gurgle which softly filled the air, notes of brawl and tumble which deafened the piteous cry of the curlews and the lapwings who wheeled and skirled on either side of the stream! "But whence?" He lay in his canoe, shut his eyes, and tried to throw himself back to the first beginnings of memory. But it did not help him. No father, no mother; not a face bending over his cradle; not an evening prayer at his bedside; ever the same Joseph Nixon, stranger in a strange land, belonging to nobody. Memory would not help him as he drifted downwards; but over his head there was the beating of wings, and the willow trees on the margin caught a sigh of the breeze as it stole down the vale, and the gurgling of the water beneath him increased and grew till his ears were filled with it and his heart was sore with it, and for very desolation of ignorance of the why and the wherefore, and the whence and the whither, his eyes became wet with tears. But that was enough for him. "Children cry for the moon," he said; "I have not been sent here to solve the problem of existence, and I have been a coward about my father and mother because I have been threatened with an origin which will humiliate my pride. I am a bastard! Well—so be it; but whose? I have been supported for years from behind the scenes. They who supported me know, and what they know I shall discover. For I am on the eve of a discovery about Mina Durie, which, if I am correct, will lift her beyond my sphere."

It is a fact that hidden secrets in science are often contemporaneously revealed to men working a hemisphere apart. They have had no knowledge of the processes by which they were each working; they have been ignorant that they were working at them at all; but contemporaneously the veil is brushed aside, and what was in the region of darkness before comes into the light. Usher and Nixon were not a hemisphere apart, and they were not working at science; but it shot into both their minds at once, or very nearly at once, that Mina Durie was the baronet's daughter. No sooner had Elspeth, her bosom heaving, and her eyes flashing, whispered to him, "Maybe, she never was aboard the ship," than the answer seemed to come, "Then is she the daughter of the absent or dead Sir Thomas Dunbeath." The difference between Usher and Nixon was, that while it filled the former with an ardent determination to secure the supposed heiress for his wife, it made the latter feel that he, who was legitimately engaged to her, must, in the case of her turning out to be Miss Dunbeath, give her up. How could the base-born look to a marriage with the proprietress of Cnoc Dhu and Ruddersdale, and all the moorlands and fields and sea-shores? No; he would not do Mina that injustice. He would be a man, and his love for her carrying him on to inquire who she was, and to find out the secret, he would go no further than to ascertain all that concerned himself, after which he would retire out of sight. Having taken off his coat to dig at Cnoc Dhu, he need not be ashamed to do it in other lands far from the dream of his first manhood. Miss Dunbeath would ascend to her proper sphere; he would gravitate to his own lowly level; he would force no debasing love upon her; he would discover all, and quietly retire. He lay in his canoe, and went down the singing Cranberry slowly, and a new-born lamb would bleat at his elbow as he passed, and the munching of the grass by moving figures in the dark told him of browsing flocks. He opened his eyes, and the lights from above were visible to him, opening up a white pathway on the stream. "Sense knows not; Faith knows not; only that it is through mystery to mystery." "Be it so," he repeated, putting out his paddle and gliding into the centre of the stream. The movement woke up a sand-martin, which went piping on the wing far down the stream before him; an otter rose with a salmon in his jaws, and disappeared with a splash; a heron flapped heavily from a neighbouring tree, and went away among the shadows of the moor; the sheep stopped browsing, or wearily shifted their position; only the light from above remained on the stream to lighten his path. He flashed by them regardless of their astonishment, neither noticing them, nor thinking of them. " Mina is Lady Dunbeath," he murmured ; " and I must give her up." Nor did his arm cease from its labours till he had got to the northernmost side of Ruddersdale, at the little bridge among the trees, whence he ascended to the high road, and returned to Nancy Harper's. Nancy's kitchen was full of the noise of laughter, inspired, he judged, by deep draughts of whisky, from the unrestraint of the men who were laughing. He went through the dark passage, and stood in the doorway. The great fireplace was red with the flames of a log, which lay sparkling above a heap of peats. Nancy's " feyther," with a tumbler in his hand, sat with his shawl about him, at the side of it. A dozen deep, there were chairs from the fire to the centre of the kitchen, and in each chair was a miner in a more or less advanced state of jollification. Armstrong was beginning to sing,

"Three potatoes for a crown, in Australia, O!" when Nixon appeared. He did not cease till he had completed six verses, when he was overwhelmed with the noise of the applause, each miner hitting his neighbour's tumbler till the hams in the rafters shook, and Nancy, who was standing apart at a dresser, arms akimbo, began to look solicitous. It was the first time the miners had come in force to her house. She was a little afraid of them, for she was used to a quieter kind of potations and to the crooning rather than the roaring of songs. She had not made up her mind, apparently, whether their patronage was to be a good or a bad thing for her.

"Hillo, there!" shouted Armstrong, catching a sight of Nixon in the doorway. "Don't stand like a skeleton at a feast. Come in. Get a cannikin, and clink, clink, clink. By the Lord, you have your eyes about you. You're the chap who'll fill your pockets before any of us has commenced. Sit down, man

make room for the chum—room, I say." And to
the right and left of his own chair Armstrong twisted
three or four chairs of his comrades, and seizing a
black bottle from the floor, passed it along to the
new-comer.

"It's song-time just now; but we're coming along
to the yarns in a jiffy—a yarn apiece, and nobody to
shirk his share. True or false—it's all one to us.
Bring him in, some of you, by the nape of the neck,
if he won't move out of that lintel."

"By-and-by," said Nixon, "when I've stopped a
gap in my bread-basket. It isn't every one of you
who's been to the top of Cnoc Dhu to-day. And I'm
hungry, Mrs. Harper, and would have a room to
myself and something solid to eat."

"You'll get that," said Mrs. Harper, following
Nixon into a little genteel room off the doorway,
where there was a small red fire of coals in a grate,
and a white tablecloth on the table, and a brass lamp
shining on a shelf.

"They're noisy, noisy men. But, poor fellows, there's no harm in them. They're just big boys, Mr. Nixon. ·I hope you'll no' find it an inconvenience, sir, their coming here to sing and drink and enjoy themselves. There's something offended them at the Duke's Arms, and they've come to me in a body. I'll no' let them go past a certain point, ye ken, for I will have a well-ordered house, as I've always had : but they're just boys."

"Mrs. Harper," said Nixon, leaning at a black shelf over the fireplace, "you once told Miss Gun, or suggested to Miss Gun, that the babe who came ashore from the foreign wreck had never been aboard of the wreck at all. That's so, isn't it ?"

Mrs. Harper put her knuckles down upon the table, steadied herself, and with a mechanical motion of her left hand drew a chair in position for herself. Mechanically she sat down. Her face wore an expression of grey decision and angry reticence.

"You said you would like a bit o' something to

eat," she remarked feebly, without looking at Nixon. "There's a cold fowl—it's cold because I was keeping it for Mr. Laggan of the mail-coach, but he went by me to-day. You can get that. I'm sorry it's cold; but you can have a warm fluke before it; and wi' that and a gill, maybe the hole in the bread-basket will fill up."

"Mrs. Harper, I don't want to annoy you in any way. But you seem to me to be evading my question. Have you any reason to suppose that Mina Durie was not brought ashore, as Sheriff Durie believes, as Roderick Leslie represents that she was brought ashore, as everybody thinks she was, Mrs. Harper?"

But the old woman only rose, left the room, brought in and set down the "warm fluke," and coming forward to the mantelpiece, put her hand on his arm, exclaiming—

"There, laddie, sit down to your meat. Eat, drink —dinna be ask, ask, askin' questions. You're here to dig : dig and eat, and be content. I'm happy to see your young face in my house, and to hear you in the passage, and to ken that you will be back to your meals; but dinna be aye ask, askin'. I'll be thinkin' ye have a purpose o' your own—that you've been sent here to my poor bield, wi' the law in your nieve—I will that, if you'll never be done saying, 'Mrs. Harper, what? Mrs. Harper, how? Mrs. Harper, is it? or was it? or do you think? or should you suppose? Take Ruddersdale as you find it, Mr. Nixon. You're but a young fine lad yet. What would you do, troubling yourself wi' mysteries? The bit lassie you talk about is well enough wi' the sheriff. The sheriff is a noble gentleman. I've given him a horn o' brandy in this very room, poor man ; and he's asked me all thae questions fifteen, sixteen, aye, eighteen years ago. Dinna be thinking, because you're young and you like the bit lassie, that all that's in your head has come into it for the first time. The sheriff has been through all the mystery before; and what's good enough for him should surely be good enough for you. Now, I'll bring in the fowl to you, for I see you're no' going to touch the warm fluke, and a cauld fluke is a dish I will not set down to anybody. Ay, the sheriff asked and asked, poor gentleman, every question eighteen long, long years ago. Put it by ye, Mr. Nixon. What matters it what a puir shepherd lassie would say to ye?"

"She is Lady Dunbeath, Mrs. Harper. She is Lady Dunbeath, and you know it, and are concealing the secret and doing the sweetest woman on earth a gigantic injustice; and out it must come, if we take it out of you in the witness-box in the Inner House. Mina Durie must go up to her high estate. She must get her own. She must ——"

"And Mr. Nixon has a little interest in the bit lassie coming into her own. Sir, I looked upon you as a man that had no great greed o' gain. Maybe you're not so disinterested as puir auld Nancy Harper supposed. No! Maybe you would like to marry Lady Dunbeath. I'm no' findin' any fault wi' your shapes and your capacities.——Coming, coming!"

There was nobody calling Mrs. Harper, but she went out, brought Nixon's fowl, laid it down, and pressed him into his chair.

"Now, Mr. Nixon, dinna you fash wi' this business," she continued, "for it's a' settled lang syne wi' Roderick Leslie; he's no' the man to be meddled wi', an' ye have a young life, an' should look to preservin' it."

"I'm not afraid of it, Mrs. Harper," said Nixon, addressing himself to his fowl; "not in the least, and I know no particular reason why anybody should want to deprive me of it."

"It's a queer coil, this world, sir, and there's accidents happen in it; and tak' my advice, and do your bit diggin', and leave all this business to God's providence to settle. I hope and trust and believe that in God's own day, if there be any heir to Sir

Thomas Dunbeath, he will be—she will be—she——
Coming, coming ! "

Without invitation, she went out of the room again. Nixon despaired of getting any information from her. He finished his meal, therefore, lit his pipe, and went down to the pier, where the sound of the sea would, he believed, be more congenial to him than the noise of the voices of the miners in their cups. The starry darkness had broken out into the half-light of a frosty segment of the moon. He leaned in his favourite attitude upon the upturned keel of an unused boat on the quay. Yes, the voice of the sea was decidedly an improvement upon the shout of his comrades, sad and unintelligible as it was, as its white waters swept the shore, and moaned, retreated, and gave forth nothing but a dull, crashing roar, and came back again in long ridges of whiteness, to moan and roar under the glittering stars and the frosty moonlight. Nixon paced the pier without interruption. He heard the village sounds behind him; he heard the bell in the village steeple ring eight; he heard men laugh in the square, and it seemed as if some of the mining glee came down to him from Nancy's window. Yet it did not give him that sense of pastoral peace which some people associate with village life remote from the turmoil of cities. Rather he had an eerie feeling that the shadow of some great mystery, which he might be destined to solve, hung over Ruddersdale. There was a mystery, and one which he saw that more than one person was concerned in concealing, and if he must pluck out the heart of it, it might be at his own peril. Else, what did Roderick Leslie mean by his fits of illness? What did the shepherd mean by his guarded silence? What did Nancy Harper mean by her kindly postponement of all definite information? Opposition to his inquiries only stirred him the more to the belief that Mina Durie was Sir Thomas's heir. "Mina, Mina! and am I set apart to solve the mystery, and to leave you for ever?"

He paced the pier till the bell in the steeple rang nine,´when a man, with an oil-skin, a sou'-wester, and a boat's rudder on his shoulder, came slowly down the quay.

"Frosty," said Nixon as the fisherman passed him.

"Ay, a wee thing."

"You're not going out all by yourself?"

"I am, though."

"To pull your lines?"

"To pull my lines."

"How far out do you go?"

"As far as a point off the Skerries."

"What do you catch out there?"

"What it's the will o' God to send me—aiblins twa-three flukes; aiblins twa-three ling; aiblins a turbot; aiblins naething. But I put mair faith in't than I do in the goold, onyway."

"I should rather like to go out with you to the Skerries."

"It's cauld, man."

"Never mind—I am used to it. The Skerries. You don't happen to remember a wreck there sixteen or eighteen years ago, in which——"

"Sit down, man, till I get this sail up. Come oot o' the bow and tak' your seat aft beside me. She'll run to the side o' the Skerries in half an hour wi' this blow o' wind. Do I remember?"

"Yes—a wreck on the Skerries eighteen years ago, and an infant coming ashore?"

"Mind your head wi' that sheet. Now sit ower to starboard; she has a list to port wi' that wind. Do I remember? Yes; sixteen—eighteen years ago, some time about then, the first steamer that ever ran between Ruddersdale and the sooth went to the bottom. Not on the Skerries, though. No; not there. The Skerries hae broken the back o' many a pretty ship, but not the *Puffin*. The *Puffin* went out with a freight o' great ladies and gentlemen—there was the Duke's butler and his wife; there was Sheriff Durie's wife and her brother, I believe, and——

Mind your head, now, till I bring her about. Yes; it was a big sink that. Now, they were all on their way sooth; and the *Puffin* was never heard tell o' again."

"The sheriff's wife? I had forgotten about that. Poor old fellow! To be sure! And it's on the altar of his affection for his drowned wife that he picked up the waif recovered from the sea about the same time."

"He's a fine, cracky, cheery man, the sheriff. He has little to do wi' altars to my knowledge. About she goes again; mind your head. My lines are down yonder—a little thing west o' the Skerries. See, a dozen or two buoys bobbin' up and doon. I think I'll get a turbot the nicht, maybe."

Nixon peered beneath the sail. He saw the surf surging over the fatal Skerries: to the west there were the buoys. The fisherman had forgotten about the wreck. Like the shepherd, he remembered scores of wrecks on the same ridge of rocks, and confused them.

"The poor sheriff," thought Nixon. "He has taken over Mina in memory of his wife. That is why he is so reluctant to part with her."

CHAPTER XIX.

A LETTER.

SHERIFF DURIE had some of his letters sent to him at Durie Den, some of them to his club in Princes Street, some of them to Parliament House, some of them to the office of a Writer to the Signet. The letters which came to his own house were usually of an inoffensive character; he chose to arrange his life so that as few annoyances as possible should meet him inside his own door. It was his theory that home was home, and should be made as comfortable as might be; his home letters, therefore, were usually invitations to dine in town, notes unconnected with the law, "how d'ye do's?" from old friends, and what not. It was with great disgust, therefore,

that he observed at the side of his plate, one morning
at breakfast, a letter from Ruddersdale in Nixon's
hand-writing. The sheriff had no intention of being
hard upon Nixon. He had failed at the bar himself,
however, and he regarded other bar failures with a
want of leniency which was more in accordance with
the laws of human nature than of logic. Logically,
he should have argued that, having been a bad
pleader himself, it was no sin and disgrace in
another man to have mistaken his vocation. But
that was not how he argued at all. Here was a
young fellow wanting to marry his ward. His ward,
he was determined, should not marry poverty.
Present wealth he did not greatly care about, but
some indication that the wooer had the power to
collect enough of guineas to make the road easy for
travelling on—that he must see. He saw it in
Usher, not in Nixon. It was rather an aggravation
to him that where he had failed Nixon also had failed.
He had no sympathy in him whatever, and he tore

the envelope, upon which he recognized his fine Roman hand, all down the back and round the edges.

"He's going to whine about his love and make a fuss about the separation," murmured the sheriff; "the less I see of him, the less I like him. Blind idiot that I was, not to notice sooner that she cared for him; the very circumstance of the man's birth being, instead of a safeguard, as I supposed, a positive attraction to her—a positive attraction!"

"MY DEAR SHERIFF DURIE—[H'm!],—I was not to write you till the strip of the deed of conveyance you gave me had assisted me to some discovery.—[No you were not.]—It has lain in my portmanteau, where I placed it on leaving Edinburgh.—[Very good!]—But I think that, in another way I have come to the outside hedge of a discovery.—[The coward! the mean fellow! He promised me he would not write her till he had found something. It is a miserable subterfuge.]—When Mina was placed in your hands you were told by Roderick Leslie that she was brought ashore from a wreck in the bay.—[Does the fellow suppose that I can't take, weigh, and decide upon evidence? He wishes to open correspondence with Mina again. I will stop his letters. No, I won't. I'll quarrel with him. I'll drop him. I'll take Mina to the Continent, and Usher to speak French for us, and trust to the chapter of accidents.] —Now, I have reason to suppose that she may never have been aboard a ship at all—that she may, in fact, have been born ashore. The suspicion—[Suspicion! H'm! That won't do. We want facts, Mr. Joseph— hard evidence. You may suspect away, my good fellow!]—has been borne in upon my mind by the remark of a shepherd-girl.—[A shepherd-girl! Ha! ha! Good—susceptible Joseph!]—She casually men- tioned—[casually! Good!]—to me that the innkeeper, Nancy Harper, had said to her on one occasion that the girl might have been born on shore.—[The chief witness. If I had not become aware in the course of years that swearing is as bad a habit as spitting, I should swear. I hate the man at this moment.]—Nancy Harper herself bids me mind my own business.—[Bravo, Nancy! Shrewd people up there. Bravo! Yes, let him mind his own business, by all means!]—But the more I think over the circumstance, the more I am inclined to think that Mina Durie is Mina Dunbeath, heiress to the estates of Ruddersdale and Cnoc Dhu."—[There is collusion here. Usher has written Nixon, and put him up to it. They are a couple of caitiffs, and my little girl would be well rid of both their attentions.]

The sheriff's little girl came down to breakfast at that moment, and looked at him with a suggestion of surprise at the tenderness of his manner. She glanced at the letter in his hand, but did not see that it was from Nixon. The sheriff put it down, with address beneath, as if it were a begging letter or a boot account, or some other written reminder of no importance whatever. But he took his breakfast very quietly, and in the middle of it stuck the *Caledonian* so that his head was invisible at the other end of the table. He was dismally supposing that if Sir Thomas Dunbeath's daughter were sitting at the other end of the table, he would lose her before long. He looked at the wall of print in front of him without reading, furtively drew Nixon's letter within it, and read and reread it ; and when Mina remarked—" Papa, dear, I don't see your face this morning," he shoved the letter into his trousers' pocket, as if he had been a schoolboy suddenly detected in exhibiting a marble or a top to a disinterested neighbour at prayer-time.

"Oh, I didn't notice that," said the sheriff. "I was reading a leader here—one of these slashing— you shall hear a bit of it."

And the sheriff began upon an article upon national finance, and went over a paragraph of it before he observed that it was not slashing at all.

"I've had a good night's sleep, but I shall yawn if you go on."

"You don't need to do that. I began on the wrong column. Here you are. That's into them, isn't it? They won't leave the poor clergy alone. Note as a physiological fact, supported by powerful statistics, that nine out of every ten clergymen, after being placed, have red noses. Got their statistics from the men at the plate. Polled the country two Sundays ago. I can't make out, however, what they deduce from the redness. Seem to believe that clergymen's wives spend their time in pulling their noses. Too fanciful to be true. Besides, what if it be true? Surely a man may be allowed to choose his own colours. It's all a question of taste."

The sheriff chipped all his eggs and devoured them, drank his coffee, and put on a disreputable hat, with the intent to stroll in his grounds. They were not very extensive, but they were well enclosed with trees; there was plenty of green grass, a good deal of

·:heery chirruping and singing of birds, and a seat in a nook here and there, where a cigar was a fine temporary reconciliation to things as they are. The sheriff lit a cigar, and again took Nixon's letter out of his trousers' pocket. He tried to smoke his way to perfect calm. He looked at the letter half-a-dozen different ways. He fillipped the envelope on to the walk, and he contemptuously rolled the letter up in a ball in the hollow of his hand, and dropped it, as if he were not giving it a thought, at the side of the seat. Then a little breeze came along and shook the myrtles opposite him, and moved the envelope and the paper ball, and he found himself pouncing upon them and restoring them to his pocket.

"She may be Lady Dunbeath, and I am robbed. I am robbed of my treasure. Meddlesome fools! What have they to do with her origin?"

He rose abruptly, went back by the stables, had his horse saddled, and rode into Edinburgh at so reckless a pace that he would have been stopped, once and again, had not the guardians of the peace recognised him *en route*. He went straight to the Writer to the Signet and handed him his letter.

"Now, freely, from reading that, without a single forethought or afterthought, what do you think?" asked the sheriff.

"That the man had better look to his own origin, and first of all find out who he is himself. He is not far away from his own origin, if Grant's account of the payments which have educated him be true."

"How so?"

"Well, Grant had these payments, if I am not mistaken, from Leslie, who stopped them lately, on the ground that the young man's people, whoever they may be, had left no more resources. The terms of the payment were, that no questions should be asked. And being asked, it was discovered or asserted that—the old story, bar-sinister—in which case the youth had his curiosity checked."

"Naturally," said the sheriff. "Yes; I know something of that, though not precisely in the terms you state. Give me a sheet of paper."

He got it, and wrote—

"DEAR NIXON,—My advice to you is, to confine your attentions to your own parentage for a little: let Mina's alone. You have not quite observed your parting promise—never to address me at Durie Den till you had done something with the strip of the deed of conveyance.

"How are my 'Eminent Scotch Sheriffs' getting along? Oh! thanks; very well. I am labouring away at the administration of Scotch law during the Reformation. Difficult question that,--very. Heard Straven's comment on Smeaton's fairies? Shut the door," etc.

END OF VOL. I.

Printed by Hazell, Watson, and Viney, Limited, London and Aylesbury

www.ingramcontent.com/pod-product-compliance
Lightning Source LLC
Chambersburg PA
CBHW051313060726

PP18533700001B/3